MAR 15 1994

GHOSTS
DON'T GET
GOOSE BUMPS

OTHER BOOKS BY ELVIRA WOODRUFF

NOVELS

The Secret Funeral of Slim Jim the Snake
Dear Napoleon, I Know You're Dead, But . . .
The Disappearing Bike Shop
Back in Action
The Summer I Shrank My Grandmother
Awfully Short for the Fourth Grade

PICTURE BOOKS

Show and Tell
The Wing Shop
Tubtime

GHOSTS DON'T GET GOOSE BUMPS

Elvira Woodruff

drawings by Joel Iskowitz

Holiday House / New York

Text copyright © 1993 by Elvira Woodruff
Illustrations copyright © 1993 by Joel Iskowitz
ALL RIGHTS RESERVED
Printed in the United States of America
FIRST EDITION

Library of Congress Cataloging-in-Publication Data
Woodruff, Elvira.
Ghosts don't get goose bumps / by Elvira Woodruff ; drawings by
Joel Iskowitz.—1st ed.
p.   cm.
Summary : Vacationing on a farm in West Virginia near the haunted
glass factory where crazy old Irwin Loop used to make marbles,
eleven-year-old Jenna decides to use the place to shock her mute
younger brother into talking.
ISBN 0-8234-1035-8
[1. Mystery and detective stories. 2. Mutism, Elective—Fiction.
3. West Virginia—Fiction.] I. Iskowitz, Joel, ill. II. Title.
PZ7.W8606Gh   1993   92-56589   CIP   AC
[Fic]—dc20

For Mr. Brunetti, whose memories of a little marble factory in the hills of West Virginia seemed especially sweet one starry night.

With special thanks to all the folks in Hollidaysburg, including Susan and Rhonda, two librarians of distinction (with very good hair).

E.W.

GHOSTS
DON'T GET
GOOSE BUMPS

Chapter One

There are two kinds of goose bumps. There are the kind you get when something bad happens, and you're so afraid, your skin starts to pucker with fear. A creepy feeling runs up your arms and across the back of your neck, sending a shudder down to your toes. That's the bad kind.

The other kind, the good kind, is when something so wonderful happens, you feel it in your bones, and your skin sends a wave of bumpy good feelings all over your arms.

The thing I like about goose bumps is you can't control them. I had never thought much about them, good or bad, until last summer when I met my best friend for life, Angel Swope.

Sometimes things don't turn out the way

you figure they will. You make all kinds of plans and in the end, none of them work out. But sometimes wonderful things happen that you haven't even planned on (a goose-bump kind of wonderful).

If our family's plans *had* worked out last summer, we'd have gone to Disney World, and I might never have met Angel, but because my dad got laid off from his job and had to start a new one, he couldn't take a vacation. So when my aunt and uncle moved to a farm in West Virginia and invited my younger brother, Nelson, and me to come and spend a few weeks, we were thrilled.

"It's not Florida, but at least you're going somewhere different this year," my dad said. Different doesn't begin to describe Three Springs, West Virginia. It is about as far away from Disney World and the America I am used to as you can imagine. There are no malls, no video arcades, no pizza parlors, and no sidewalks. What's there instead are roosters crowing in the morning and fireflies flickering in the cornfields at night. There are ponds of croaking frogs and trees full of bluebirds.

My aunt and uncle's place has a little old

house with a falling-down barn and a bunch of sheds and chicken coops out back. There is a worn path in the weeds leading from the house to a weathered blue outhouse surrounded by big golden sunflowers. Nobody uses the outhouse, as there is a real bathroom in the house. Next to the outhouse is the "family pool," a big, old-fashioned bathtub that Uncle Mark painted purple.

Uncle Mark works as a mason. He wears brown overalls that are covered with cement dust, and his big, heavy work boots are usually caked with mud. He's got twinkly blue eyes and a reddish brown beard. His stomach is so big that when he laughs, you can watch it go up and down. Uncle Mark laughs a lot, and so does Aunt Shelly, only her stomach isn't big like Uncle Mark's. She's got curly brown hair and big strong hands that aren't afraid to open a horse's mouth or to reach under a chicken for an egg. Before she had my cousin, Jack, Aunt Shell worked as a horse trainer.

Wherever they live, they always have animals. At their new place they have three dogs, six cats, two horses, nine pigs, twenty chickens, and three ducks. Only half of their one hundred acres is cleared for fields; the rest has gone to woods, honeysuckle, and wild rose. They named their new place Freedonia Farm, and I loved it the minute I saw it.

We hadn't been at Freedonia long, when my aunt Shelly gave me fifty cents and suggested that Nelson and I walk down the road to Peachy's, the only store in Three Springs, for ice cream.

"They have just two kinds," Aunt Shell told us, "Creamsicles and Nutty Crunch cones." Nelson and I had never been to a store that only sold two kinds of ice cream, and we weren't too eager to go, but Aunt Shell insisted.

"Go on, you won't be sorry. Those Nutty Crunch cones are the best."

My parents had gone back to New Jersey by this time and they wouldn't be picking us up till the end of the month. A month is a long time to go without ice cream, so Nelson and I followed Aunt Shell's directions and walked down the long driveway, turning onto the gravel road. Peachy's was a short walk away.

Peachy's turned out to be a little general store with one rusty gas pump outside and three short aisles inside. The shelves were crammed full of stuff from the floor to the ceiling. They sell everything there from diapers to gunpowder. The owner, a tall cornstalk of a man whom everyone calls Peachy, lives with his mother in a house attached to the store. Their kitchen door opens onto the aisle with flyswatters and bananas.

When I first saw Peachy, I thought he should have called the place String Bean's, since he looked more like a string bean than a peach. It didn't take me long to look down all three little aisles and find the store's only freezer in the corner. Nelson, who doesn't like nuts and is so-so about Creamsicles, stopped to check out some squirt guns. I headed for the freezer and the Nutty Crunch cones. That's when I first saw her, my soon to be best friend for life.

I knew right away that Angel Swope was different. I guessed that she was about my age, although she wasn't dressed like me or any other eleven-year-old girl I knew. Her shorts were bright purple and her top looked like it was once an Indian dress that had been cut in half. It was a faded green color, with tiny little

mirrors sewn all over it, and bands of purple
embroidery around the arms. She had a long
ponytail of thick black hair, and on her freck-
led nose sat a pair of large, blue-rimmed
glasses. The lipstick she had on was the same
color red as her high-top sneakers. But that
was only how she looked on the outside. What
was really different about Angel was what came
from the inside.

As I stepped up to the freezer, she turned
around. I could feel her looking me over as I
peered into the case of frozen vegetables and
pizzas. I soon discovered that you had to dig
if you wanted an ice cream from Peachy's
freezer.

"My name is Angela Swope, but my television name is Angel Always," a confident voice
announced. "All my friends call me Angel, and
you can, too."

I turned around and smiled. I had never
met anyone who had been on television before. I stood staring, wondering what a TV star
was doing in a place like Peachy's.

Chapter Two

It took me awhile to get up the nerve to ask, "What show are you on?"

"You're not from around here, are you?" Angel's voice had a definite twang. I shook my head. Angel frowned and adjusted the blue glasses on her nose. I couldn't help but notice that there was no glass in the frames.

"I haven't been on any shows yet," she explained, "but it's only a matter of time before I get discovered, because I've got actin' in my blood." She threw back her head with a satisfied grin.

"Are your parents actors or something?" I asked.

"No, my daddy's a welder and my mom works for a dentist over in Orby, cleanin' folks' teeth," she said matter-of-factly.

"Orby?" I didn't know what she was talking about.

"Orbizonia. It's the nearest town, but it's a mouthful, so folks round here just say Orby," Angel explained.

"How do you have acting in your blood?" I asked.

"Because I was named after the soap star, Angela Harris, of course," she said. "And when you're given someone's name" (she lowered her voice here), "it's the most soulful gift you can ever receive, because a part of them is in your soul and always will be. Who are you named after?"

I shrugged. "I don't think I was named after anyone," I told her. "My mother just liked the name Jenna."

"Oh, that's too bad," Angel said. "Maybe you could get a good nickname."

I had lived for eleven whole years without once thinking about the origin of my name, yet suddenly the name Jenna Connerton seemed woefully unsoulful. I felt as if I had been deprived of one of life's great gifts.

"Don't worry, nicknames can be just as good," said Angel. She reached into the freezer, pulled out two Nutty Crunch cones, and handed one to me (without my even having to ask). I grinned as a wave of goose bumps broke out on my arms.

So began the unlikely friendship of Angela "Angel Always" Swope of Three Springs, West Virginia, and me, Jenna Connerton, soon to be nicknamed Pearl Amelia Anastasia Connerton, and finally just plain Jenna Pearl, of Summit, New Jersey.

It didn't take me long to find Nelson. He hadn't budged from where I'd left him. He was shining his flashlight on a bright orange water gun. (Nelson got a big red flashlight for Christmas last year, and he doesn't go anywhere without it, day or night.) I quickly explained that we didn't have enough money for a squirt gun and that if he didn't want a Creamsicle, I'd buy another Nutty Crunch for myself. I don't think Nelson really wanted the Creamsicle, but I could see from his face that he didn't want me having two of anything he didn't have. I ended up going back to the freezer and digging out a Creamsicle for him from under some bags of broccoli.

Paying for the ice cream proved to be even

more of a challenge than finding it. No one was at the little register up front, or back at the meat counter either. Angel finally closed her eyes and took a deep breath.

"Smell that?" she said. I took a whiff of air and definitely smelled something cooking, although I couldn't tell what it was.

"That's pork roll," Angel said. "Peachy's probably cookin' some up for himself and his mama. They take a late lunch on account of the store. We can just leave our money on the counter. You don't need a polk, do you?"

"A polk?" I didn't understand.

"A polk," she said, pointing to a stack of paper bags.

"Oh, no," I told her, "I don't need a bag." She gave me a funny look as we laid our money down. I followed her outside to a wooden bench facing the gas pump out front, and we both sat down. Angel started right in, bombarding me with questions about my life back in New Jersey.

"Tell me everything," she demanded, "from the day you were born." I tried to fill her in as best I could, and within ten minutes she was coming up with nicknames.

"Pearl would be good, because pearl is your birthstone and Pearl Buck was a great writer. She wrote about China. Granny Wheeler has all her books. Do you like Chinese food?"

"I like fortune cookies," I said, biting into my Nutty Crunch.

"Or how about Amelia?" Angel suggested. "There's a beautiful girl called Amelia on one of Granny's soaps."

"I did a report on Amelia Earhart last year in school," I announced proudly.

"How do you feel about flying?"Angel asked. My shoulders slumped. I wasn't crazy about airplanes, although I did like the name Amelia.

"Oh, I know!" exclaimed Angel. "Anastasia. I saw a show on TV about her once. She was the youngest daughter of the czar of Russia."

"That's a pretty long nickname," I said.

We went on and on like that, and by the time we finished our cones, Angel was calling me Jenna Pearl, which seemed to fit the best. It felt like we had been friends for a long, long time.

As Angel and I sat out on the bench talking, I looked around for Nelson. He was over by the road, trying to give part of his Creamsicle to Peachy's scrawny black cat, Jasper.

"Nelson, you get away from the road," I warned.

He looked up, nodded, and stepped back onto the grass.

Angel pushed her glasses up on her nose, tilted her head forward, and gave Nelson a long look. This was the part I always dreaded. Whenever we met new people, they would stare at Nelson and then ask, "What's wrong with him? Why doesn't he talk?"

"Nelson's not like other five-year-olds," I said.

"I can see that," Angel mumbled.

"Why?" I said. "Because he doesn't talk?"

"No," Angel replied, "because he's got distinction."

"What's that?" I asked.

"It's a special look or way some people have about them. It sets them apart, makes them special somehow. It's what you need to have if you want to be a soap star, that and good hair," Angel explained. "There was an article called 'Stars of Distinction' in my granny's soap digest magazine last month."

I sighed. "I don't know about any of that stuff, but I guess he does have good hair. And he's a pretty good brother. He isn't a pest like some brothers are. Nelson loves animals and he's always kind and gentle with them. He just doesn't talk, that's all."

"He's got distinction, that's for sure," said Angel, swatting a fly off her arm. "Hasn't he ever said anything, though?"

I shook my head. "Not one word. My parents have dragged him to dozens of doctors, but they can't find anything wrong with him. Everyone's got his own theory of why he won't talk, but no one seems to know why for sure. My parents are sending him to a special school next year. I heard my mom crying about it in her bedroom."

We sat swatting flies for a while, as the scent of pork roll and ketchup filtered through the store's screen door. And for the next two weeks, Angel and I spent nearly all our time together, except from one to two-thirty in the afternoon, when she went over to her granny Wheeler's house to watch soaps. Angel watches soaps in the summertime the way most other kids watch cartoons. I asked if I could go along, but Aunt Shell didn't think my parents would approve. I was allowed to go to Peachy's for a Nutty Crunch cone every day after lunch, though, as long as I took Nelson along.

Angel didn't have money for a cone every day, so I usually shared mine with her. As soon as we finished eating it, she'd take off to get to her granny's in time for the soaps. One afternoon, while we were sitting out front on the bench watching Nelson shine his flashlight in Jasper's ears, Angel got this funny look on her face.

"I wonder what he sounds like," she said.

"Who?" I asked, licking the drops of ice cream off my hand.

"Nelson," she whispered. "I wonder what his voice sounds like."

I had never thought about what Nelson might sound like if he could talk. I was so used to not hearing him, I almost couldn't imagine him with a voice.

"You'd have about as much chance of hearing Nelson talk as you would Jasper, there," I told her. That's when I noticed the funny glint in her eye.

"I just thought of something wonderful,"

Angel whispered. "Wouldn't it be wonderful if . . ." She paused and her smile widened, so that her teeth were now showing.

"If what?" I demanded.

"If we could get him to talk!" Angel exclaimed.

"Who?"

"Nelson, of course," whispered Angel. "Now, wouldn't that be wonderful?"

"Sure," I agreed, "it *would* be wonderful if Nelson could talk, but how are we supposed to get him to do it?"

"Well, I was watching this soap the other day . . ."

"Here we go again." I sighed. Angel was always talking about her soaps.

She slid over on the bench until she was almost sitting on top of me. Her gray eyes grew bigger and bigger behind her blue frames as she continued to whisper in my ear.

"It was on the show 'All Our Days.' This beautiful lady, Courtney, didn't talk either. She was about to leave her house to go to the hospital to have a baby, and when she opened her front door, she found her long-lost daddy, who she thought was dead, standing there. She was so shocked, she fainted. Her daddy called an ambulance and she was rushed to the hospital. She had a baby girl, and when the nurse brought the baby to her, she looked down with tears in her eyes. She said, 'Oh, my beautiful baby!' Those were the first words she had ever spoken in her whole life, and everyone, the doctors, the nurses, and her family stood by her bed, laughin' and cryin' at once. My cousin Denise, my granny Wheeler, and me were sittin' on Granny's couch, in front of the TV, gettin' all teary-eyed, ourselves."

"Well, I don't think Nelson is ever going to have a baby," I said.

"It's not havin' the baby that did it, silly." Angel groaned. "It was seein' her long-lost daddy. The doctor on the show explained to Courtney's family that a shock of some kind can trigger somethin' in a person's brain, and they'll suddenly be able to do somethin' they have never done before, like talk, or walk."

"So what are you saying?"

Angel rolled her eyes. "Jenna Pearl, you are dense! Don't you see? All we have to do is give Nelson a shock of some kind, and he will be talkin' up a storm by this time tomorrow. I think they call it shock therapy or somethin'. I bet he's got a wonderful laugh. Just imagine how glad your folks would be if they could hear it."

Angel was so confident and enthusiastic, I couldn't help but feel excited myself. And like a true friend, she went on to announce that she would give up watching her soaps for the day, so she and I could "organize a plan of action for Nelson's shock therapy."

We sat in silence and stared at our future patient, who was gently stroking Jasper's stomach. Angel was right. Nelson does have a special look, with his dark hair and gentle smile. I tried to imagine what his voice would sound like if he could talk. It would be soft and gentle, not high or screechy, I decided. His voice would match his look of distinction. Talk about wonderful! I could just picture my parents' glowing faces when they heard him laugh for the very first time.

"But there's one thing we'll have to decide from the start," Angel broke into my daydream.

"What's that?" I asked.

"We'll have to decide whether to give him a good shock or a bad shock," she whispered.

Chapter Three

We continued our conversation on the walk back to the farm, keeping our voices low so Nelson, who was busy kicking a stone a few yards ahead of us, couldn't hear.

"If it were a bad shock," I whispered, "how bad would it have to be?"

Angel adjusted her glasses. "Probably not as bad as lightnin' strikin' him," she said. "Maybe just a good jolt would do it, like the kind you get when you touch a light switch with wet hands."

The roots of my hair tingled at this suggestion.

"Or it could be a frightful kind of shock," Angel mused. "Seein' somethin' like a grizzly bear or that hairy monster Bigfoot."

"Oh, great!" I groaned. "And just how do

you plan on getting in touch with Bigfoot?"

"I don't suppose he'd be in the phone book, huh?" Angel giggled. We discussed other shock therapy treatments for Nelson, everything from putting snakes in his bed to sticking spiders down his back.

"But if we put snakes in his bed," I said, "I'd get such a shock from touching them myself, *I* might stop talking for the rest of *my* life. Everything we've thought of for scaring Nelson would scare me as well."

As we turned off the main road to the driveway, Nelson ran ahead of us. We were almost to the house when Angel spotted a bluebird.

"Look, it's on that tree right there," she said, pointing. "It's really blue."

But the only color I could see was green. "I see the tree, but I don't see any bluebird," I mumbled, squinting in the tree's direction.

"Here," said Angel, taking off her glasses, "maybe these will help." I put them on.

"Nope, I don't see it," I told her. I squinted some more and rubbed my eyes inside the glasses frame.

"You know, Angel," I said, "the thing about glasses is the glass. The glass is a special lens that helps you see better. Without the glass, glasses don't really work." Just then I spotted something blue out of the corner of my eye and saw the most brilliant bluebird I had ever come across in my life, perched in the tree.

"I see it!" I cried.

Angel grinned. "Good thing you were wearing the glasses or you might have missed it." I started to protest, but she was quick to stop me.

"I know all about the glass and the lens," she said. "But sometimes it doesn't work that way. Have you ever heard of the power of suggestion? You believe in somethin' enough and the impossible becomes possible. It's the believin' that makes it all happen. It's what actin' is all about. A great actress is like a magician. When people watch her, they're convinced that what's happenin' is real. She makes them feel glad or sad."

"I guess I never thought about it that way," I said, handing the glasses back.

"Besides," Angel continued, "I don't wear these glasses for me to see, I wear them for people to see *me* differently. They give me distinction, don't you think?"

I was about to answer when she pointed to the tree again.

"Maybe that's the bluebird's nest," she whispered. She went over to the tree and, standing on tiptoe, gently lifted out a small nest.

"Are there any eggs in it?" I asked, leaning over her shoulder to have a look.

"Well, if these are birds' eggs, I'd sure like to see the bird that laid them!" Angel exclaimed. She pulled out two perfectly round, sparkling glass spheres.

"They look more like marbles than eggs," I gasped. "What are they doing in there?"

"I don't know," Angel mumbled, holding up one to the sunlight. "I never knew a bird that could lay a marble before. And look at how they glow. They sure don't look like ordinary marbles." She handed one to me and I shivered at its touch.

Just then Aunt Shell called, "Come and have a swim." I could see her with the hose, filling up the old bathtub in the backyard. Tootie, Aunt Shell's smallest dog, was sitting on a lawn chair watching her. Tootie is a yappy little thing with black corkscrew curls all over her.

She loves to follow my three-year-old cousin, Jack, around the farm. Nelson was pulling off his shirt. Within minutes he and Jack were climbing into the tub.

"Why don't you girls take a dip when the boys are through?" Aunt Shell suggested. "You have an extra bathing suit Angel can wear, don't you, Jen?"

Tootie started yapping and then jumped into the tub with a splash.

"Tootie's in the tub again, Mom." Jack shrieked with laughter.

"Oh, Tootie, not again," Aunt Shell scolded. "You must be the only dog in history who volunteers to take a bath! Come on, Tootie, you'll have to wait until everyone else is out." Nelson grinned and Jack hooted with laughter as Aunt Shell pulled a soggy, dripping Tootie out of the tub.

"Aunt Shell," I said, after she had flopped down in a lawn chair, "look what we found." I held up one of the marbles.

"We found two in a bird's nest along the driveway," Angel added.

"Marbles in a bird's nest?" Aunt Shell was as surprised as we were. "They're so unusual-looking," she added. I nodded in agreement.

Angel adjusted her glasses. "Do you think they could have somethin' to do with this once being old Irwin Loop's place, before you bought it from Crombies?"

"Maybe you're right. It was the Loops who ran the marble factory down in the hollow, wasn't it?" Aunt Shell asked.

Angel nodded.

"A marble factory in Three Springs?" It was the first I had heard of it. "Did they make real marbles?" I asked. "The kind kids play with?"

"They used to," Angel replied, "but that was a long time ago, before I was born. Irwin Loop ran the factory after his daddy, Thadeus Loop, died. Old Thadeus Loop was making marbles down there when my granny Wheeler was a bitty girl. The factory shut down a long time ago. But even after all those years, that holler is still known as Marble Holler, and there are folks that claim it's haunted."

"Haunted? How?" I asked, cupping my hand over the shimmering marble.

"Well," Angel began, "you can still see the old factory. It's nothin' more than a little brick building, sitting way down in the holler, all

overgrown with weeds and such. Irwin Loop
and his sister, Neva, ran it for a while, but
they shut it down when Irwin took sick. A few
years back, a girl from around here disap-
peared, and they found her jacket down in the
holler next to the old factory. That was all they
ever found of her. My daddy's got a strict rule
that I'm not allowed anywhere near the holler
without a grown-up along, though it don't
seem very fair since my brothers get to hunt
there all the time."

"I think your daddy's rule is a good one,"
Aunt Shell said. "Whether there's a ghost or
not, I don't think you should be playing around
those kinds of lonely places. That goes for you,
too, Jenna."

"I wouldn't want to go there anyway, if it's
supposed to be haunted," I said. "Has anyone
seen the ghost of the girl?"

"No, no one's actually seen the ghost. Most
folks think it's the ghost of old man Loop himself that snatched up the girl. They say if you
happen by the holler on certain nights, you
can hear the glass grinding machines going,
and see smoke from the furnace. They say the
ghost of old man Loop won't rest. And that

every now and then he comes back to haunt the place, hopin' to make up a new batch of marbles."

"Angel, you watch too much television." Aunt Shell shook her head.

"No, ma'am, I mean, yes, ma'am," Angel said. "But I don't like the ghost stories. They give me too many goose bumps. I stick to daytime viewin' only." Aunt Shell and I had to laugh.

"You can laugh all you want," Angel said later after we'd changed into our suits and were sitting alone in the bathtub. "But you still can't explain what those marbles were doing up in that bird's nest, unless . . ."

"Unless?" I asked, slipping farther into the cool water.

"Unless they aren't ordinary marbles," she whispered, "made by an ordinary person." I sat up a little and looked over the edge of the tub. The two marbles lay on a towel in the grass. I don't know whether it was the cold water in the tub or the sight of those strange shimmering marbles that sent goose bumps down my arms.

Chapter Four

Later at supper, we showed the marbles to Uncle Mark.

"They sure are the strangest marbles I've ever seen," he muttered. "Maybe they did come from old Irwin Loop's factory. We bought this place from the Crombies two months ago," Uncle Mark pointed out. "And before they owned the place the Loops lived here for a long time. Irwin Loop must be in his seventies now, and he was born here."

"Why did he leave?" I asked.

"He lived here alone for the last few years," Uncle Mark explained. "According to the neighbors, he wasn't in his right mind for a number of those years. That's why his sister took him in and why he's living with her now. Well, Angel, you've probably heard the story."

"Yes, sir," Angel spoke up. "Old Irwin Loop, he never hurt a fly, but he was touched in the head, all right. His sister, old Miss Neva, has been lookin' after him in a little shack she rents from Peachy's cousin Wilson. She's got to look after him 'cause he can't be left on his own. Couldn't string more than three words together for a sentence."

"So it's likely he could have gone around the place doing things as crazy as putting marbles in birds' nests," Uncle Mark concluded.

"But they don't look like ordinary marbles," I insisted.

"That's probably because they were made so long ago," Uncle Mark said. "The glass they used must have been different."

"Maybe," Angel said softly, "but I wouldn't be so sure."

We talked for a while longer about the Loops and the haunted marble factory, until Aunt Shell changed the subject. She asked Uncle Mark to tell us about the tractor auction he had been to earlier in the day.

"Well, let me see," Uncle Mark began, "there was one pig farmer named Nick who had a long white beard and a big round belly, just like Santa Claus." Jack leaped up on his chair and said, "Santa Claus is coming!"

Nelson held his white napkin to Jack's chin so that it looked like a beard. Uncle Mark said, "Ho, ho, ho," Jack said. "Ho, ho, ho," and everyone laughed. But we all got real quiet when Jack turned to Nelson and said, "Nelly, you say ho, ho, ho." Nelson smiled and reached over to tickle Jack. Jack began to laugh and tickled him back, and he soon forgot all about the ho, ho, ho.

But Angel and I didn't forget. We were both eager to get to work on our plan to shock Nelson into talking. So after getting Aunt Shell's OK, Angel called her mother and asked if she could spend the night. We knew that once we were in bed, we could stay up for hours talking about our plan. For a treat, Uncle Mark said we could sleep on the little screened-in porch off the kitchen.

"It's actually our most-sought-after suite at Freedonia Farm," Aunt Shell said, her voice taking on a snooty tone. "The views of the compost piles are extraordinary, and for truly fine dining, the hog shed is just a walk away."

Angel and I giggled as we shoved two cots

together. Aunt Shell gave us pillows and sheets and one big quilt to share. The small screened-in porch was perched on a slight angle, so we felt like we were hanging off the house in a little boat anchored to a much larger ship. A gentle breeze blew through the wind chimes hanging from a hook in the corner. We spent a long while whispering under the soft quilt, while the cinnamony aroma of peach cobbler drifted through the kitchen window. That night in the cozy private world of the rickety little porch, amid the chirping of crickets and the tinkling of wind chimes, Angel and I made promises that we'd be best friends for life.

"And instead of friendship rings, we'll have our marbles," Angel said.

"We can carry them with us wherever we go," I whispered, "so we'll never forget how special we are to each other." Angel smiled as we tucked our special marbles under our pillows, then sat up. We looked through the screen at the sky and saw the first star of the night. Angel suggested we make a wish.

"I thought you only made wishes on falling stars," I whispered.

"You can wish on whatever you want," Angel said. "I don't think it's what you're wishing on as much as the way you're feelin' while you're wishin'. If you're feelin' really good, the goodness will reach the wish."

"Did you hear that on one of your soaps?" I asked.

"No," Angel said, "I just know it."

I looked up at the dark sky and fixed my eyes on that one lone twinkling star. The lightning bugs had begun to flicker above the weeds.

"I wish that we could get Nelson to talk," I whispered. "I wish I could hear his voice."

"Me, too," Angel said, reaching for my hand. "Let's close our eyes and wish as hard as we can." So I shut my eyes tight, and squeezing Angel's hand, I wished again. We sat there silently, wishing for a long time. When we opened our eyes, the apple tree was glittering with the twinkling lights of hundreds of lightning bugs.

"Will you look at that!" Angel gasped. We didn't say anything for a long while. Then we both lay back on our pillows, watching the tiny lights going on and off in the woods.

"I'm covered with goose bumps!" I said, looking down at my arms.

"Me, too," Angel said. "These are the best kind of goose bumps, the kind you get when something really good happens."

"It's so beautiful, I feel like I'm in a dream," I whispered. "I've never seen so many lightning bugs."

Angel yawned. "Last night I stayed up till almost midnight. My little brother Pete and I opened our window, and with the screen up, we kept catching the fireflies that were flying into our room."

"Is that what you call them?" I asked. "Where I come from we call them lightning bugs. I like fireflies better. That's what I'll call them, too."

"Have you ever had any in your room at night?" Angel asked.

"No," I answered. "My mother doesn't like us to lift up the screens."

"Neither does mine, but I always leave them open jest a crack, so the fireflies can get in. Ever catch any outside in a jar?"

I shook my head. "My mother doesn't like us going out in the yard after dark either," I explained.

"That's too bad. They're fun to catch," Angel replied. Suddenly she sprang up and cried, "That's it!"

"What's it?" I asked.

"Nelson's shock!" she exclaimed. "It just hit me. It doesn't have to be a bad shock. We could give him a good shock instead!"

"Like what?"

"Like he could wake up in the middle of the night to a roomful of fireflies or lightnin' bugs or whatever you want to call them. A whole roomful!" Angel spread out her arms.

I knew that Nelson liked lightning bugs or fireflies, and I had to admit that the idea of waking up to a roomful of twinkling lights would make him feel pretty good, but good enough to talk? I wasn't sure.

"What do we have to lose?" Angel asked. "If he still won't talk, at least the fireflies will make him feel good. Besides, you gotta catch a firefly at least once in your life. It's too wonderful an experience to miss. And tonight's the perfect night."

So we had our plan. We would sneak into the kitchen and find some jars, then sneak outside and catch as many fireflies as we could.

We'd sneak into Nelson's room, let them loose, and wake him up. It sounded like a lot of sneaking, but I figured it was better than putting snakes in his bed.

Ten minutes later we were in the kitchen, grabbing one of Aunt Shell's big canning jars. Uncle Mark and Aunt Shell were in the living room playing cards with some of their friends. We placed a piece of tinfoil over the top of the jar and Angel poked some holes in it with a fork. I was about to reach for a second jar, when we heard someone coming.

We rushed back onto the porch, grabbed our sneakers, and then ran outside. Soon we were running through the grass in our night-gowns, with arms outstretched and hands grasping at the rising clouds of twinkling bugs. Everything seemed so different in the moon-light. The trees, the house, even the old bath-tub looked magical. I took a deep breath, sucking in the perfume of honeysuckle and jack pines.

"I'm in a dream. This is better than Disney World," I whispered to Angel, who was bend-ing down in the grass. She stood up and dropped three fireflies into the jar.

"Uh-huh," she agreed. "And these fireflies are flying so slow, they're a cinch to catch. Let's not stop until we have the whole jar filled. Look, there's a bunch of them over there," she said, pointing to another cloud of flickering lights beyond the barn. We took off, and before we knew it, we were chasing fireflies farther and farther from the house.

"Jes' a few more," Angel said, when I suggested we turn around and head back. A few more and a few more after that led us deeper into the woods.

I was beginning to worry. What if we got lost? It would be worse than being lost at home, where you could stop at a gas station or a restaurant to use a phone. There were no phone booths in these woods, just trees and more trees, and they seemed to go on for miles.

I couldn't help thinking about the conversation I had heard the other day at Peachy's. Boyd Meekum had claimed to have spotted a wildcat up on the ridge. Peachy himself said he saw a fox not ten feet away from the store. It was not the kind of conversation I was used to hearing. We don't usually see foxes or wildcats in Summit, New Jersey. I clutched Angel's nightgown as she came to a stop.

"It's OK, Jenna Pearl," she assured me, "we're not lost. I know right where we are." Then she took off in the opposite direction, with me trudging along behind. It wasn't long before she came to another stop, only to start off again in still another direction.

"I was a little confused," she said. "Don't worry, Jenna Pearl, I know right where we are. We're not lost."

After an hour or so, my worrying began to turn to panic. Meanwhile the moon was dipping in and out of the clouds, causing monsterlike shadows to appear all around us. The leaves rustled over our heads and an owl began to hoot in the distance.

Angel came to another stop beneath a tangle of vines, and my worst fears were realized when I heard her whisper, "Jenna Pearl, I'm sorry to say this, but I don't know where we are. I think maybe we're lost."

Chapter Five

"Oh, no!" I whimpered. "What if we come across a fox, or a wildcat, or Bigfoot!"

"Don't worry," Angel assured me as she flopped down beside a tree. "I'll figure a way out. And if we run into Mr. Bigfoot" (her voice was wavery with fear), "we'll just play dead."

"Play dead!" I cried, falling down beside her.

"Yeah, it's what you're supposed to do if you run into a grizzly bear," she explained.

"Grizzly bears!" I squeaked. "Are there grizzly bears here, too?"

"Not too many," Angel whispered. "But it's lucky I've been studying to be a soap star for so long. I know all about playing dead. I watched Tiffany die on 'One Bright World' just last week. It's not hard."

"Oh, great," I moaned. "And did Tiffany die in the middle of some forest with Bigfoot and grizzly bears attacking her?"

"Well, no," Angel muttered. "Actually, she died in Brent's arms at his lake house. Brent was her old boyfriend. Her new boyfriend was Rick, but it wasn't until she was dying that she realized she loved Brent more . . ."

"Angel, we're lost!" I cried. "We may be about to die, and all you can talk about is some stupid soap. Are you loony or something? This is not 'One Bright World' we're in. This is One Dark Woods!"

I couldn't see her face very well in the dark, but from the sound of her voice, I knew she was hurt.

"I am not loony, Jenna Pearl, I am an actress," she said. "And soaps aren't as stupid as you think. There is a lot of real-life stuff going on in them."

"I'm sorry, Angel," I apologized, "it's just that I'm scared."

"Me, too," she admitted, "so let's not be fightin'. We need each other right now." We huddled closer together as the wind whistled through the trees overhead.

"What if we never find our way out?" I moaned, shuddering.

"They'll send a search party," Angel replied, adjusting her glasses. "We shouldn't be thinkin' the worst, though, Jenna Pearl. Try and think about somethin' else," she advised.

"Does that sound like a bear to you?" I whispered. Angel tilted her head to listen and then shook her head.

"Naw, that's a frog croakin'," she answered, jumping up. "If there're frogs around, there must be water. Listen, do you hear that?" she asked. She started walking toward some low bushes. I followed, listening to the sound of water rushing over rocks. Angel grinned as we approached a stream.

"All we have to do is follow this crick and it'll lead us out," she announced. "I know this crick. It runs through the holler to the road. It's easy to get back to the farm from there."

A wave of relief washed over me. We followed the twists and curves of the creek as it wove its way through the woods.

"When we get to Marble Holler, we can take the road back to your aunt and uncle's place," Angel suggested.

"Is that the same Marble Hollow that you were talking about today?" I asked. "The one with the old marble factory? The one that people say is . . ."

"Haunted," Angel finished my question. "Yep, that's the one."

"Haunted." My skin puckered into goose bumps at the sound of the word. I didn't want to talk about anything being haunted while we were still out in the middle of the woods, but Angel persisted.

"Do you believe in ghosts, Jenna Pearl?"

"I'm not sure," I mumbled, trying to ignore the fact that it had grown much darker in the thickest part of the woods. An umbrella of gnarly vines was hanging above our heads. The sweet smell of honeysuckle had been replaced by the damp, cloying scent of moss and rotting wood. After what seemed like hours we came to a clearing.

"We must be on the edge of the holler," Angel whispered over her shoulder. Then she stopped so suddenly that I almost walked into her. The canning jar began to slip from my hands, and the tinfoil fell off into the grass.

"The jar!" I cried. But Angel was pointing

ahead. I followed her gaze to the outline of a little brick building rising out of the weeds in the moonlight. Three small windows caked with dirt and grime glowed from within. My ears began to tingle as a buzzing, whirring sound filled the air. I could feel Angel's fingers digging into my arm at the sound of glass being crushed. I hardly noticed the flurry of twinkling lights escaping from the jar in the grass as my eyes fixed on the building's wobbly old chimney, and the thin curl of smoke winding out of it.

"It's . . . it's . . ." The words were sticking in my throat.

"Loop's old marble factory," Angel whispered.

"And it's . . . it's . . ."

"Haunted!" she croaked. "It must be haunted! Jenna Pearl, do you believe what we're seein'? We're watchin' a ghost at work!"

My knees began to buckle beneath me.

"Let's get a little closer, maybe we can see inside," Angel said, taking a step forward.

"Now I know you're crazy!" I cried. "Why would we want to do that? I thought you hated watching ghost stories on TV."

"But this isn't TV," Angel whispered. "This is happenin' right now, in real life, right here in Three Springs. And no one else has ever seen him up close. . . ."

"Him?" I gulped.

"You know, the ghost, old Thadeus Loop. If we saw him," she added, "we could probably get our pictures in the Orby *Gazette*. We might even get to be on one of those talk shows on TV. People who see ghosts are on them all the time. Just think, Jenna Pearl, this could be my first TV appearance. All we have to do is get a little closer and look through one of those windows."

"I don't think I can move," I whispered. "I feel like I'm frozen to this spot."

"Do you want to wait here *alone*, while I check it out?" Angel asked, taking another step forward.

"No," I whimpered.

"If we can get close enough, we can look inside," Angel whispered, taking my hand. My heart was about to jump out of my chest. Slowly we made our way forward. When we finally got to within inches of the building, we ducked behind some bushes to hide. I buried my head in my hands.

"Don't you even want to look?" Angel whispered.

"You look for me," I croaked. I peeked through my fingers. She was leaning around the bushes. Even though I was shaking with fear, I was curious, too. I pushed myself up.

"The windows are so dirty, it's hard to see in, but there's definitely someone in there," Angel reported. "I can see the shadow of something moving around." She leaned forward.

"What else?" I asked.

"There's one little corner of the windowpane that's cleaner than the rest," Angel said. "I can see a chair, and a long wooden stick of some kind, with a snake carved around it. I think it's a walking stick, with the snake's head at the handle. There's a shiny green marble in the snake's mouth. And there are these really old wrinkled fingers reaching for . . . Yikes!" she screamed. "It's the fingers of the ghost! I see the fingers of the ghost!"

We sprang up, and with Angel in the lead, we flew out of the bushes and along the creek until we came to the road. We didn't stop running until our feet hit the gravel of Freedonia Farm's driveway.

As Angel slowed a bit to catch her breath,

she cried, "The hand was wrinkled up and the fingers were all yellow and gnarly-lookin'. Like the hand of someone who's been dead for years and years. And the arm was long and skinny with lots of goose bumps all over it."

"Goose bumps?"

"Yeah, at least they looked like goose bumps," she said.

"I never heard of a ghost getting goose bumps," I told her.

"I never did either," Angel admitted. "But then I never saw a real ghost before."

"Could you see through the fingers?" I asked. "The way they do in the movies when they see a ghost and can see right through them?"

Angel's forehead wrinkled as she thought this over. "I'm not sure. It happened so fast. I might have, but I can't say for sure. But that walking stick was definitely strange. I read a Halloween story about a witch who had a walking stick. It reminded me of that."

"I wonder what Aunt Shell and Uncle Mark will say about all this," I mused as we came around by the house.

"Jenna Pearl, you don't plan on tellin' them,

do you?" cried Angel, taking hold of my arm.

"Well, sure, it wasn't like we went there on purpose or anything. If we hadn't gotten lost we would never have . . ."

"We can't tell anyone," Angel insisted.

"I thought you wanted to tell the world," I reminded her. "Remember, your first TV appearance and all that?"

She made a face. "Now that I'm thinkin' about it, it's not such a good idea."

"Why not?"

"Because my daddy's got a real bad temper. And if he finds out that we went chasin' fireflies in the woods at night, and got so lost we ended up in the holler, he'd throw a fit. He'd take away my TV watchin' for a month. And he'd make me stay home, so I wouldn't even get to see you for the rest of your visit here."

"I guess my aunt and uncle wouldn't be too happy about it either," I said, looking at the porch. "Aunt Shell did tell me not to play there."

So we agreed to keep our night in the hollow a secret, and with it the ghost of Thadeus Loop. I was so exhausted from our adventure, my eyes began to close the minute we got back to the porch and under the quilt. Angel, on the other hand, was excited. She rattled on and on about ghosts, and marbles, and witches' walking sticks, until I couldn't keep my eyes open any longer. The last thing I heard her say was, "And poor Nelson. Those fireflies would have been such a great shock. I wonder what he would have said if he had seen all those twinklin' lights. Just imagine it, Jenna Pearl . . ."

I drifted off to sleep with my hand under my pillow and my fingers wrapped around my marble. I must have been smiling in my sleep, since my dreams were full of fireflies and the sound of laughter. It was a soft laugh, not high or screechy, but soft and gentle and full of distinction.

Chapter Six

When we woke up the next morning, I felt as if we hadn't even slept. Angel started right in on "the ghost in the holler." We lay in bed, whispering, until Aunt Shell called us in to breakfast.

"I know, don't tell me," she said, when we dragged ourselves into the kitchen, "you two were up half the night talking, right?" Angel cracked a smile, and we both nodded.

"I'm placing you on berry detail," Aunt Shell said, setting out our cereal bowls. "Company is coming for the weekend, and it would be nice to make a berry pie." She told us about the family that was about to visit. They had been friends of Aunt Shell and Uncle Mark for years and years. I wasn't paying too much attention, since my mind was on other things, namely ghosts.

Later that morning, Angel and I bent over the wild raspberry bushes growing along the driveway.

"I've never been so scared in my whole life," I said, pulling a handful of berries off a bush.

"And we thought seein' Old Bigfoot was goin' to be scary," Angel mumbled through a mouthful of berries.

"If you keep putting all the berries in your mouth, instead of in the bucket, we'll never get enough for a pie," I told her.

"I can't help it. All that fresh air last night gave me a big appetite."

As I reached for a long branch covered with berries, Angel shouted, "Look out. There's a mess of stingin' nettles in there."

I looked at the light green bushes growing around the berries.

"They're bushes with tiny little stingers that grab onto your skin and leave you all bumpy and stung up," Angel explained. "It's nothin' you'd want to mess with, believe me."

"Does it last a long time? The stinging, I mean."

"Naw, you can't die from the pain, if that's what you mean," she said. "And you can usually find a pokeberry bush nearby. The juice from the stems of pokeberry is the best thing to put on the stings. Clears them right up. I get into nettles all the time on account of playin' in the fields."

"I hate for so many good berries to go to waste," I said, staring at the branch.

"Better they go to waste than you go crazy with nettles. Besides, the birds need their share of berries, too."

I decided she was right, and left the branch and the stinging nettles untouched. We went on picking awhile longer.

"I still can't get over that ghost." Angel sighed. "I never thought I'd really see one."

"Hopefully it will be the last one you see," I replied.

"I'm surprised my hair didn't turn gray or somethin'. When some people have a shock like that, their hair can . . ." Her voice trailed off. Her mouth dropped open, and she looked at me.

"Oh, no," I said, rolling my eyes to the sky, "don't even think it."

"Why not?" she cried. "All Nelson has to do is take one look at the ghost, and he'll have to say somethin' about it."

"What about us?" I protested. "I don't think

I could take another shock like the one I had last night. Besides, I thought you said your father would be really mad if he found out. And what about my aunt and uncle?"

"So who's goin' to tell them?" Angel whispered, reaching for another berry. "Jenna Pearl, as you are my best friend for life, I feel it is my obligation to help you in your time of need."

"My time of need?" I muttered.

"With your little brother, who you care so much for."

"Good grief." I groaned. I closed my eyes, and I could see us on "One Bright World." Not only did Angel talk about her soaps all the time, she sounded like them, too.

"It's not the time for me to be thinkin' about myself," she continued in the long-suffering voice of a daytime heroine. "Nelson is your brother, and he needs our help. And if that means riskin' hearin' my daddy holler and gettin' locked up in the house for a month . . ." She paused here for the proper dramatic effect. "Then I would risk it." Her eyes lit up. "Besides, if we can get Nelson to talk after seein' the ghost, we'll be heroes. My daddy would be too proud to be mad. Oh, Jenna Pearl, can't you just see it? They would love us on the six o'clock news." Her voice got lower as she imitated the serious tone of a TV announcer:

"Tonight I'm happy to report that two brave girls risked their lives to hunt down the supernatural apparition that has long tormented the good people of Three Springs, West Virginia. Giving little thought to their own safety, and thinking only of the welfare of a small five-year-old boy, these two courageous girls faced unspeakable dangers. We're going to take you to Three Springs now, for live coverage of the amazing event that changed the lives . . ."

"Don't you ever give up?" I groaned, pulling another berry from a bush.

"Of course I'd have to get a new outfit, somethin' in purple, 'cause purple is my best color," Angel went on. "And I'd get some of that mousse stuff for my hair. I'd have to get my hair lookin' real good. . . ."

"Not in a million years am I going back to that hollow." I raised my voice. "Do you hear me? Not in a million years."

"You don't have to shout." Angel winced as

she popped another berry into her mouth. "But what about Nelson?" she insisted. "Think about Nelson."

"I am thinking about Nelson, and I know my parents would never want us to go to that place alone with him at night."

"Maybe you're right," Angel muttered. "We could use some reinforcements right about now."

"Reinforcements?" I sighed. "Angel, we aren't going to war, and we aren't going back to that hollow."

"But what if someone else went with us?" she pleaded. "Would you go then?"

"Like who?" I asked.

"I don't know," Angel said, scratching her head. "But would you go, just tell me that?"

"Maybe," I said. "If they were older, and if . . ."

"Great!" She grinned. "Now all we have to do is find somebody, quick."

She was about to say something else but the loud honk of a horn made us jump. We turned around to see a blue van making its way up the driveway. It slowed to a stop, and a smiling woman in the front seat rolled down her window.

"Looks like a good day for picking," she said. She introduced herself, and I realized that this was the company that Aunt Shell had told us about.

"You must be Jenna," she said to me. "You look just like your aunt Shelly. I'm Mrs. Brisson and this is my husband, Mr. Brisson." She nodded to a rumpled-looking man behind the steering wheel. "And our four boys." She began pointing to the boys in the backseats. "Zachary is twelve and Ben is eight. Noah's six, and that's Gabriel, our baby."

Angel and I looked at the boys and smiled. None of them smiled back, except the baby. This didn't stop Angel.

"I'm Angel Always, and this is Jenna Pearl," she said, pointing at me. I was glad she had introduced me like that. I was feeling good about my special nickname, but I hadn't met too many new people in Three Springs I could use it on.

"Ma," one of the younger Brissons wailed, "Zack shot me with his water gun again!"

I looked into the backseat and saw one of the older boys drop a water gun. Everyone dove for it. Amid the tangle of arms and legs and brown hair, a green plastic water gun emerged and took aim. It fired at Mr. Brisson's ear.

"That's it!" Mr. Brisson yelled, swatting the side of his head with his hand. "Out! Out of the car. All of you, get out!"

"Now, dear." Mrs. Brisson's smile had faded, and a strand of her straight brown hair had fallen over one eye. "We're almost to the house," she whispered.

"I don't care," her husband huffed. "After four hours in the car with these kids, I can't take another minute. Out, all of you. Out! You can walk the rest of the way!" He turned around in his seat and pointed to the back door. Angel and I stared at the van door as it opened. Three Brisson boys tumbled out. The baby smiled and waved from his car seat. Mr. Brisson stepped on the gas and the van pulled away in a cloud of dust, heading for the house.

"What are you two looking at?" one of the boys growled in our direction.

"Reinforcements," Angel whispered in my ear, "and they couldn't have shown up at a better time."

Chapter Seven

"What are you talking about?" I whispered, not taking my eyes off the boys. They were edging closer to the bushes.

"You said you'd go if we had someone to go with, so here they are," Angel whispered back. "We don't need all of them. We'll wait and pick out the bravest." The three boys had begun grabbing at and tearing into *our* raspberry bushes, shoveling berries into their greedy mouths as fast as they could.

"What do you think you're doing?" I demanded, planting my hands on my hips.

"What does it look like?" smirked Zachary, the oldest.

"These bushes are private property," Angel said. "Jes' because you're visitin' doesn't mean you can come along and help yourself to whatever you like."

"So how come you get to pick them?" Ben, the eight-year-old, asked.

"My aunt and uncle own this farm," I told him.

"And we were asked to pick them for a pie," said Angel.

"Maybe if you had some glass in those phony glasses of yours," Zachary taunted, "you'd see what you've picked. Doesn't look like you did a very good job." He lowered his eyes to our nearly empty bucket. It was probably a good thing that Angel's glasses were glassless, because the look she shot Zachary Brisson would have melted any glass in those frames. But when he turned and leaned closer to the stinging nettles, her expression changed.

"I wouldn't go pickin' in there, if I was you," she said sweetly.

"Why not?" asked Zachary.

"There's a mess of stingin' nettles in there and I'd hate to see you all stung up." Her face was a mask of concern. He hesitated, staring first at the tangle of leaves in front of the bushes, then at the branches with fat ripe berries.

"She's just saying that, Zack, 'cause she

didn't get to them first," Ben shouted, rushing to his brother's side.

"That looks like the best bush around," Noah, the younger one, added. He took a step toward the bush, but Zachary was quick to pull him back.

"Wait," the older boy commanded. "If anyone goes in, it'll be me." He glared at Angel, and I knew just what he was thinking. Was she telling the truth? Or was she just trying to scare him away?

Zachary stepped all the way into the stinging nettles and Angel let out a whoop of laughter. Zachary Brisson let out a whoop of his own, but he wasn't laughing. He danced around on the driveway, swatting at his bare legs. Just then we heard Mrs. Brisson calling to her tribe.

Angel and I followed them down the driveway toward the house. The sun was hot and we needed a drink of lemonade. We figured it'd be best to get to the refrigerator before the company did. "So much for reinforcements," I said.

"I don't know about that," Angel said.

"What do you mean?" I asked.

"Well, that older boy, Zack, he wasn't so bad, really. I think he might be the one to go into the holler with us."

"Are you kidding?" I cried. "After what he said to you about your glasses? I saw the way you looked at him. That was hate at first sight if I ever saw it."

"I don't think I'd call it hate," Angel said. "Besides, I got back at him. No, I'd say he's the one we should take along with us. He's got distinction, all right."

"Distinction? I didn't see any distinction," I muttered.

"There're two things that struck me about him, right off," sighed Angel dreamily. "Two very good things."

"Oh, really?" I asked. "And what were those?"

"Did you see the way he looked out for his little brothers? He could have sent them in after those berries, but he went in himself. That took courage." I stood watching as she snapped off some branches from another bush.

"Now what are you picking?" I asked.

"Pokeberry. It would be too mean not to offer him any," she explained.

"So what was the other thing?" I asked. "The other thing that was in his favor?"

Angel stood for a minute with an armful of pokeberry branches as she stared down the driveway. "Good hair," she said wistfully, "he has real good hair."

Chapter Eight

"**G**ood hair?" I cried. "What's that got to do with helping us in the hollow? We're talking about a ghost, Angel. You know, the supernatural kind. I don't think they care too much about hair, good or bad."

Angel spent the rest of the walk back to the house trying to convince me why she thought Zachary Brisson should accompany us to the hollow.

"I told you, not in a million years," I said, shaking my head.

"But you said 'maybe,' if we had someone to go with us," she insisted.

"I said someone older."

"His mother said he was twelve. That makes him older," Angel pointed out.

"I meant more than a year older." I sighed.

"Many years older, like a grown-up. Your dad and Aunt Shell are right. It's not a good idea to be going down there alone without a grown-up."

"What grown-up is going to go into the holler looking for a ghost in the middle of the night?" Angel whined.

"None, so you can forget the whole idea."

That's as far as our conversation got, since we had reached the house and Aunt Shell and Mrs. Brisson were clucking over Zachary and his stung-up legs. Angel marched right up to them and handed them the pokeberry branches. She broke off the soft stems of the plant and began to squeeze out the juice.

Speaking in a calm voice, Angel lectured the little group about the "magical medicine" of plants and herbs, including pokeberry.

"My granny Wheeler says that there's an herb to cure every hurt," she continued. She carefully swabbed Zachary's leg with an open stem. It was obvious that she had watched enough nurses on "One Bright World" to act the role of a modern-day Florence Nightingale. Angel Swope had acting in her blood, all right.

After a few minutes Zachary admitted that his legs felt better. As Angel and I headed indoors, the phone began to ring. I took off for the kitchen and picked up the receiver. Granny Wheeler was on the line. She wanted to talk to Angel.

Miss Nightingale talked to her grand-mother, while I poured myself a glass of lem-onade. Aunt Shell had invited the grown-ups into the kitchen for "a cup of coffee," so I took my drink out to the porch steps to wait. That's when I heard a voice snicker, "I said 'What's your name?' Are you so dumb that you don't even know your own name?" I looked over and saw Nelson and Jack sitting in the sandpile playing with Jack's trucks. Ben and Noah Brisson were standing inside the pile, kicking sand with their sneakers.

"Go on, tell us your name," Ben Brisson ordered.

"He's Nelly," little Jack said. I cringed as the two older boys laughed.

"Not only is he too dumb to talk, but he's got a girl's name!" they taunted. Then Ben, the eight-year-old, grabbed Nelson's flashlight and laughed.

"If you want it, ask for it back," he smirked, kicking sand onto Nelson's leg.

Nelson's lower lip began to tremble. He glared down at the sand. I was about to jump up and go to his rescue, when Zachary appeared.

"What's going on?" he asked.

"Nothing," Ben said. "We're just fooling around."

"He took Nelly's flashlight," Jack protested.

"Give it back, Ben," Zachary ordered.

"I told him he could have it back if he asked for it," Ben said. "It's not my fault he can't talk."

"Give it back, *now*," Zachary ordered. Ben shoved the flashlight into the grass. Jack sprang up and pointed at a box turtle making its way slowly across the driveway. He and the rest of the boys took off, leaving Nelson behind. He was sitting perfectly still, the truck in his hand and some sand covering his leg. A big tear rolled down his cheek. I raced over to him.

"It's OK, Nell," I whispered in his ear, "they're just bullies. Who cares about them, anyway?"

He looked up at me. As usual, I understood what he was thinking. Nelson and I had never needed words. I knew all his expressions, like the way his left eyebrow went up when he was surprised, or the way he sucked in his bottom lip when he was trying hard to figure something out, or the way he tilted his head back and grinned when he was really happy.

He wasn't happy now, though. His eyes were sadder than I had ever remembered and they were speaking to me loud and clear.

"I care," they said. "I care when other kids make fun of me and call me dumb and stupid."

"I know," I whispered, placing my arm around him, "I know."

I decided to take him into the house for a glass of lemonade. Nelson loves lemonade, and I was hoping I could talk to Aunt Shell about what had happened. But when we walked into the kitchen, it was still full of grown-ups.

"Why isn't he out playing with the other boys?" Aunt Shell asked. "And why does he look so sad?"

"He's just thirsty," I said. "He wants some lemonade." I didn't have the nerve to say that the Brisson boys had been mean and were making fun of him. I was glad when Uncle Mark reached over and scooped Nelson up into a big bear hug.

"Heck, I bet he weighs more than Biscuit," Uncle Mark joked, lifting Nelson onto his lap. (Biscuit is Uncle Mark's prize pig, and she weighed six hundred pounds when she was last put on a scale.) I haven't sat in Uncle Mark's lap for a long time, not since last year, but I remember how good it felt when he wrapped his strong arms around me and laughed his low growly laugh. Nelson tilted his head back and smiled. As much as I wanted to talk to Aunt Shell, I could tell it would be awhile before I could get her alone, so I went outside to wait for Angel on the porch steps.

I could hear the Brisson boys' voices out in the barn. They were laughing and hooting and calling to one another. The happier they sounded, the sadder I felt.

By the time Angel got off the phone and joined me on the steps, I was convinced we had to do something about Nelson. I told Angel about the incident in the sandpile.

"And that kind of thing is going to keep happening if he doesn't learn to talk," I said, fighting back the tears. "I know why my mom was crying. Nelson is the best kid in the whole world, but other people don't see him that way. They see him as dumb, as a freak. I couldn't stand it if his feelings got hurt again. I hate having him grow up thinking he's stupid."

"He doesn't have to," Angel whispered, putting her arm around me.

"But all those doctors tried, and none of them could help him. None of them could get him to talk."

"We've got something better than doctors," Angel said, pulling her marble out of her pocket.

"You mean the hollow?" I croaked. She nodded. "Alone? Just you and me and Nelson?"

"If we have to," she replied. "Unless we take a certain someone along." She turned to look at the Brisson boys walking out of the barn. Zachary was leading the group.

"I still say he's got distinction," she whispered in my ear. "He could have made fun of Nelson along with his brothers, but he didn't, did he?"

I had to admit she was right.

"He's proven to us that he's courageous and he's fair and he's a whole year older. He'd be the perfect one to come along."

"But how are we going to convince him?" I frowned.

"With this," she said, holding up the marble. "What boy can resist marbles, and we're offering him a chance to see the factory where they were made, not to mention a ghost. If he's got any distinction at all, he'll jump at the chance to come along."

I wasn't so sure I agreed, but Angel was determined.

"When?" I asked.

"Tonight," she whispered, "definitely tonight."

Chapter Nine

Later that day, Angel asked Zachary if he'd like to come with us to pick more berries. After a little prodding from his mother and Aunt Shell, Zachary said he would go. The other Brisson boys were headed for the backyard. Aunt Shell had made up a dishpan of bubble solution, and she was handing out old orange juice cans for them to use as blowers. Soon everyone was busy making bubbles and jumping in and out of the tub. I almost wished we could stay and fool around with the bubbles, but I knew that was kid stuff and that what we had to discuss with Zachary was more important.

As we walked up the driveway, Angel stopped at the nest where we had found the marbles. She reached into her pocket and pulled out her marble. Holding it up for Zachary to see, she told him about finding it in the nest. I went on to explain about Loop's factory and how old Irwin Loop had gotten gradually crazier while he lived on the farm.

"He may be crazy now but he sure knows something about making marbles," Zack said, turning the marble over in his hand. "These are awesome. Maybe he hid more than just the two you found. Have you looked anywhere else? In the barn? Or in the sheds?" We had to admit that we hadn't thought of that, but Angel quickly explained that we had been too busy thinking about the ghost. At the word ghost, Zachary's eyes grew wide.

"You're not afraid of ghosts, are you, Zachary?" Angel asked.

"I've never met one," he replied, "so I don't really know." I liked his honesty and also the way his hair curled over to the side just right. I was beginning to think maybe Angel was right. Maybe Zachary Brisson had more distinction than I had realized. We went on to tell him all about our sighting in the hollow and about Nelson's problem, and about how we were planning on taking him back with us tonight.

"You can come with us," Angel said matter-of-factly. "Do you think you'd like to go?" I held my breath as I watched Zachary kick a stone on the driveway. I was beginning to worry that he might not agree. Finally, he said, "It sounds kind of scary." He gave us each a look that told us he knew we needed him. Then he said, "Let me see that marble." Angel handed it over. Zachary held it up, staring at it for a long time.

"This is the best marble I've ever seen," he murmured. "I'll go, under two conditions."

"What are they?" Angel asked.

"That I see the factory in the daylight, first."

"But the ghost probably won't be there in the daytime," Angel protested.

"I don't know if you saw a ghost or not, but I know I've never seen a marble like this before," he whispered. "And it would be great to get some for my collection. If the factory made marbles, there must be some lying around. We could see better in the daytime and then go back at night to see your ghost, if that's what it was."

"It was a ghost all right," Angel told him. She glanced at me and without discussing Zachary's condition out loud, we nodded to one another. When you're best friends, you can decide on things without having to say a word.

"OK," I said, "we'll take you there in the daylight."

"What's the other condition?" Angel asked.

"That you call me Zack," he replied. I could see Angel melting.

"It's a deal, Zack." She blushed.

"So, when do we go?" he asked.

"Right now," Angel answered.

"Right now?" I gasped. The thought of going back to the hollow, even in the daytime, gave me the shivers.

"Now is the perfect time," Angel said, moving away from the driveway. She picked up a cornstalk to use for a walking stick. As we made our way through the cornfield, I had an uneasy feeling in the pit of my stomach.

In the daylight, Angel knew where to go, and in a short time, we came to the creek that flowed into the hollow. We stood, skipping stones and talking about the ghost. Angel seemed certain that we wouldn't see it during the day.

"You must be thinking of vampires. They're the ones that sleep all day and come out at night," Zack said. "I never heard of ghosts doing that, too."

"Well, I don't know about all ghosts, but I know this one has never been seen in the daytime," Angel replied. "My big brother Ricky and his friend Tommy Lee go turkey hunting in the holler all the time. They've seen lots of turkeys, but never a ghost, not in the daytime, anyway."

I turned to look at Zack. "Do you think ghosts get goose bumps?"

"No, I don't think so," he answered.

"But you've never seen one," Angel reminded him, "so you can't say for sure."

"Well, I just hope Nelson sees one tonight, with or without goose bumps," I said, skipping a stone that skidded four times across the water. We skipped a few more stones, since both Zack and Angel were determined to beat my four skips. Angel finally did, and we took off once more.

Marble Hollow in the daylight looked almost as mysterious as it had in the moonlight. The weeds were long and silky, and great swags of reddish-green poison ivy vines hung from the trees like showy Christmas decorations. Two gold-and-black orioles flew over our heads as we walked through a field of flowers that resembled snowflakes and tiny orange and gold fairy slippers.

"Are we almost there?" Zack groaned. He sat down to take a stone out of his sneaker.

"We've got a little ways to go yet," Angel said. She picked one of the snowflake flowers and put it in my hair. While we waited for Zack, Angel and I picked more flowers and tied them together to make a crown. Angel undid her ponytail, and I carefully placed the flowers on her head.

"How do I look?" she asked, stepping back. I blinked, unable to believe my eyes. She was wearing her same old Indian blouse, the one with all the mirrors on it, but somehow it looked different as the sun bounced off the mirrors, causing them to sparkle and twinkle as she moved. Beneath the crown of lacy white flowers, her hair seemed blacker and more velvety, and her skin looked creamy white (except for the freckles on her nose).

"You look like a snow queen," I whispered. Even Zachary stared at her as she pulled up an old weed stalk, then turned and marched into

the middle of the field. In a regal voice she declared, "I am Queen of the Hollow, and all creatures within my realm live to serve me." I stared in awe. She was using her TV voice and it was working! Why hadn't I ever noticed how beautiful she was? But it was more than just the way she looked. It was the way she sounded. Her voice was confident, commanding, and hypnotic. She was no longer Angel Swope of Three Springs, West Virginia. She seemed bigger and brighter than ordinary life.

"As Queen of this Hollow, I decree . . ." Zack and I were hanging on her every word. "I decree that . . . Oh, darn it, all these chigger bugs are bitin' up my legs somethin' fierce!" she hollered, bending down to scratch her legs. That was it. The spell was broken. She looked at Zachary and me and started to laugh. Her crown slipped to the side of her head.

"You two could both catch a mess of flies with your mouths open like that."

Zack instantly shut his mouth and scrambled to his feet. I think he was too embarrassed to admit that he had come under her spell. I couldn't help grinning.

My best friend, the actress, I thought.

We took off again, but I was so busy thinking about Angel and her spellbinding performance, that at first I didn't see the old wooden sign hanging from a rusty hinge.

"LOOP'S MARBLES INC." Zachary read the words out loud. "It doesn't look that scary," he commented. This last remark was met with a cackle of laughter from a big black crow that was perched on top of the building's crumbling chimney.

Chapter Ten

"We'll wait here while you go in and look for the marbles," Angel suggested. I nodded quickly, hoping Zack would agree. He didn't.

"If I'm coming back here with you tonight, you've got to go in with me now," he demanded. For someone with such good hair, he seemed to be a little short on courage.

We walked slowly up to the front entrance, but the door was bolted. A poison ivy vine clung to the overhang. I swallowed, trying to ignore the fear that was tugging at me.

It's just an old building, it can't hurt you, I kept telling myself, but try as I might, I couldn't shake the feeling that we were in danger.

"Let's try the back," Angel said finally. We walked around to the rear of the building.

There we found another door that was boarded over. Zachary tried to pull off a piece of wood, but it wouldn't budge. He tried opening some of the windows that were at ground level, but they were all locked.

"Looks like we won't be able to get in," I said.

"Hold on," Zack called, walking over to a window that was broken. "If I can break this glass a little more, I can get my hand through and unlock it." I held my breath as he picked up a small rock and smashed the glass. He reached through the hole, and after some struggling was able to undo the lock.

"Oh, great! I can lift up the frame," Zack exclaimed. The window wouldn't stay up by itself, so he propped it open with a stick.

There was nothing else to do but follow him through the window. It was a small opening and we had to squeeze our way in. I went first, followed by Angel.

As Angel stepped onto a table below the window, the window crashed behind her. The loud bang echoed through the room. Angel jumped quickly to the floor and huddled next to me.

"My . . . my . . . shirt must have caught on the stick," she stammered.

Shafts of light from the dust-covered windows zigzagged through the maze of cobwebs that hung around us. My eyes traveled over the silent machinery covered in layers of thick dust.

"Are you afraid of spiders?" Angel whispered.

"No," I croaked.

"You're lucky," she said.

"No, not really," I told her. "It's not the spiders, but the cobwebs that give me the creeps!"

"They can't hurt you," Zachary said. For a moment, I almost believed that he wasn't afraid.

"They're just cobwebs, and cobwebs can't . . . Ahh! It's got me! It's got me!" he cried, walking into a thick web. Angel still had the old cornstalk she'd picked up in the field. She used it to dust the cobwebs from Zack's head.

"This place is too creepy," I whispered as I saw some mice scampering into the shadows. "We should get out of here."

"There's nothing in this room but a bunch of old dusty machines," Zack said. "It's not so bad."

"Jen's right," Angel whispered. "I can't see what's wrong, but I can feel it. There's something not right about this place. Let's get out of here."

"We haven't even looked yet," Zack protested. He began searching under tables.

"Look at that one machine," Angel whispered, pointing to the corner.

"What about it?" I asked.

"There's no dust on it, like on the other machines," she said. "And no cobwebs."

We took a step closer to inspect it.

"Oh, cool," Zack exclaimed, "this must be a mold for the marbles! They melt the glass and then they pour it into these round holes," he said, running his fingers over the smooth black steel.

"That must have been the mold that the ghost was using," I mumbled.

Angel turned her head, looking at the back of the room. "And there's the furnace, where he heated the glass," she said excitedly. "And see, it doesn't have any dust on it either."

"That doesn't prove anything," Zack said, walking over to the big hulk of rusty metal in the corner. "Maybe the spiders don't like making their webs here, maybe . . ." His voice suddenly trailed off as he laid his hand on the furnace. "That's funny," he whispered.

"What?" Angel and I asked.

"This furnace. It's warm!" Zack gulped.

"Of course it's warm," Angel exclaimed. "The ghost was usin' it last night. Now do you believe us?"

"I don't know what to believe, but I do know that something weird is going on," Zachary muttered. "Let's find some marbles and get out of here quick."

It was obvious that Zachary Brisson had a one-track mind. Even with all the evidence pointing to a ghost, he was still thinking about marbles! We searched around the machines and under the tables, but there were no marbles in sight.

"Hold on, let me get out my flashlight," Zachary said, digging into his pocket. He pulled out the tiniest flashlight I had ever seen.

"That's not much better than a match," Angel complained.

"Even Nelson's flashlight is bigger than that," I said.

"It's better than nothing," he replied, shining the little wisp of light into the shadows.

"Let's face it, Zack," Angel said, "there aren't any marbles in here, so can we go now?"

"Angel's right, Zack, let's get out of here," I said, climbing up on the table. I picked up the stick and looked out the window.

Soon we'll be back at the farm, I thought. Safe, out of the hollow and out of danger. As I began to open the window, I heard a loud crash behind me. I turned. Angel and Zachary had fallen off the table, landing together in a heap on the floor.

"Are you all right?" I called to them.

"I'm OK," Angel said. "My sneaker was untied and I tripped over . . . Hey, wait, what's this?"

"What's what?" I asked.

"These floorboards are loose," she said, peering at the floor. "And look, one of them has a funny little mark painted on it in the corner."

"Come on, you two, who cares about floorboards," I groaned. "Let's get out of here!"

But they didn't budge. They didn't even look up at me. Angel sat staring at the floor, and Zack took out his penknife.

"What are you going to do with that?" I called.

"I want to see what's under here," he answered, prying the board up with his knife.

"Wow!" he and Angel exclaimed. I put down the stick.

"It's a door!" Zachary cried. I jumped to the floor.

"A secret trapdoor!" Angel cried. They were right. It was a trapdoor, with a long wooden handle. I backed away, since it didn't take much for me to figure out what was under that door.

"The ghost!" Angel whispered. "I bet he lives down there."

"You still don't have proof that it was a real ghost," Zack said.

"I don't know how much more proof you need," said Angel.

"OK," I whispered, turning back to the table, "we found out where the ghost lives, so let's not bother him. Let's get going."

"But I don't believe in this ghost business,"

protested Zachary. "And this may be the secret door leading to a stockroom or something. It might be where the marbles are stored. There could be tons of marbles down there."

"If you think we're going down there, you're crazy." Angel shook her head. "I'm not going to go waking up any ghost."

Zack frowned. "OK, I'll go down alone," he said, "but you've got to at least wait here for me." I stood thinking this over. I didn't like it, but I hadn't liked the idea of coming to the hollow in the first place. If it weren't for Nelson, I wouldn't have agreed to any of it.

"OK, we'll wait for you, but hurry up," I told him. Angel and I climbed on the table, so we'd be ready to escape quickly through the window, if we needed to. I don't know whether it was bravery or lust for the marbles that gave Zachary the courage to pull the handle and lift up the secret door. I barely had the courage to look. Peeking through my fingers, I could see a set of old stone steps leading into a dark cellar.

"You couldn't get me down there in a million years," I whispered to Angel. She nodded, and we inched closer to the window.

That's when we heard the first noise coming from outside. It sounded like twigs breaking, followed by a swishing sound in the weeds. The noises were getting louder. Someone was coming closer! Angel and I ducked below the window with our backs to the wall.

"If I had a nickel for every goose bump popping out on my arms, I'd be a millionaire," Angel croaked.

"Maybe we should call down to Zack," I whispered in Angel's ear.

"It's probably just a dog or a rabbit," she whispered back.

"Right," I muttered under my breath. I was about to relax, when I heard a loud rap at the window. Suddenly little bits of broken glass from the hole were showering down on our heads. All I remember is Angel's scream as we looked up and saw the ghost's walking stick poking through the broken glass of the window.

Chapter Eleven

I don't even remember jumping off the table, but I guess we did, since the next thing I knew we were running down the steps to the cellar to find Zachary.

"The ghost!" Angel cried, slamming the trapdoor behind us.

"He's coming in the window!" I screamed, running to Zachary. I was moving so fast, I ran smack into him.

"What are you saying?" he whispered in the darkness. "Did you see it again?"

"Yes, well, no," I stammered. "We didn't actually see the ghost, but we saw his walking stick."

"He poked it through the . . ." Angel began. "Shh . . . listen." We sat in the darkness, the clicking of our chattering teeth growing louder and louder as we heard a door open overhead.

"We've got to get out of here," Zachary finally whispered, shining his tiny flashlight around the room. His fingers were trembling so much, the little flicker of light from the flashlight wobbled up and down. Clinging to Zachary, Angel and I stepped forward. The sound of footsteps overhead gripped us with fear, and then everything went black.

"I dropped my flashlight!" Zack cried.

"Find it, quick!" I gasped.

"Hurry," Angel whispered as he reached down and picked it up. We held our breaths as he fumbled to turn it back on.

In the tiny ray of light we could see big wooden barrels and crates of glass and marbles lining the walls. Behind one of the crates, we noticed a small doorway. We didn't stop to think about what to do next, since the loud creak of the trapdoor sent us running toward the small door. We frantically shoved aside the crate and turned the rusty handle of the door. Much to our surprise, it opened, and we found ourselves looking into a long dark tunnel. We had no other choice but to enter it. We had to go single file, though, as it was only wide enough for one of us at a time. Zack went first, followed by Angel, and then me. The air, what little there was, was damp and musty.

"Don't stop, Zack," Angel called.

"The ghost is behind me!" I cried. "I can hear footsteps behind me!" We started running so fast, I thought my heart was going to explode. We ran until we couldn't run anymore. Finally, after what seemed like hours, Zack began to slow down, Angel and I did the same, until we all came to a full stop. No one spoke; we stood clinging to one another, catching our breaths, and listening for footsteps. "Maybe he's stopping, too," I gasped, my voice echoing off the tunnel's walls. We stood listening for awhile longer, but heard nothing.

"I don't think he's behind us anymore," Angel whispered.

"That's good." I sank to the ground to rest.

"Or maybe it's bad," Zack said, slumping next to Angel. "Maybe whoever is up there has tricked us into running in here."

The thought of being trapped in that black, musty tunnel was too terrifying to think about.

"Our families will never find us," I moaned.

"Our parents could search for years and never find us down here."

"They won't be looking alone," Zack said. "They'll call in the police."

"That would be Kenny Runion and his cousin Dewy," Angel informed us. "My daddy says the two of them t'gether need a map to find their way out of Peachy's. They spend most of their time there, struttin' under their turkey feet."

"Turkey feet?" I repeated. Could she really be talking about turkey feet at a time like this?

"Uh-huh." Angel nodded. "Over at Peachy's, on the wall behind the toilet paper and paper towels, there's a mess of turkey feet and turkey beards hangin'. Every time somebody gets himself a bird, they bring the feet and the beard down to Peachy's, so they can show them off on the wall. Kenny and Dewy's got the most feet of anybody. My daddy says they spend more time huntin' down gobblers than they do criminals."

"Well, if the police don't find us, my mother will probably call in the FBI," Zack said. "My mother is the biggest worrier there is."

"The FBI would be good," I said, trying to

cheer myself with the thought of hundreds of FBI agents scouring the woods for us.

"At least the FBI doesn't spend all its time hunting turkeys," Zack remarked. "They've got all kinds of tracking devices, sonar and even infrared stuff."

"But then again, I don't know about the FBI." I frowned. "What about all those kids on milk cartons and on the news? Why can't the FBI find them?"

"Listen, we don't need any old FBI or any fancy sonar stuff," declared Angel.

"We don't?" Zack sounded doubtful.

"No," Angel told him, "we've got Hootz."

"Hootz?" Zack and I both repeated.

"He's my brother Ricky's coon hound. Hootz's got the best tracking nose in the county. He can tree a coon faster than any dog alive, least that's what Ricky says."

"I wonder how long it'll take them to figure out we're missing?" I said. As we talked about being rescued, I noticed that Zack was beginning to wheeze with every breath he took. Angel and I watched as he shined his flashlight in his pocket and pulled out a white plastic bottle with a nozzle.

"What's that?" Angel asked. He held it in his mouth and took a few deep breaths, his chest heaving up and down.

"It's my inhaler," he told her, sitting back against the wall. "I've got asthma, and when I get an attack, I need to use an inhaler to help me breathe."

"Can I try it?" Angel asked.

"Sure," Zack said, handing it to her. I really would have liked to have tried it, too, but I was afraid that asthma might be catching.

"There was a high-school girl in our town who died of asthma last summer," I said. "Do you ever worry about dying?"

"No," Zack replied. "I've got the inhaler, but if I get really bad I get a shot at the doctor's office." I was about to question him further, but another sound came from down the tunnel.

"Do you think it's the ghost?" Angel whispered.

"It's coming from the wrong direction," Zack remarked.

"And it doesn't sound like footsteps," I added. We sat listening some more.

"It sounds like scratching or digging, the

kind of noise a rat or a mole would make," said Angel, jumping up.

"I hate rats!" I winced.

"Yes, but if it's an animal, that must mean there's an opening to this tunnel," Angel suggested.

"It might only be big enough for a rat to get through, though," Zack remarked.

"Maybe," Angel admitted, "or maybe not. If our folks do find us, it's not going to be for a long while, so we might as well see what's at the end of this thing. Come on."

"Aren't you afraid of stumbling onto a rat?" I whispered as we continued down the dark tunnel.

"Naw," she answered, "they can smell us comin'. They'll get out of the way. Zack, do you need your breathy thing back?" she called to him.

"No, not now. I'll get it when we stop again," he answered. Angel shoved the inhaler into her pocket. We walked for a long time. Just as I was about to suggest we sit and rest, Zack let out a loud whoop.

"What is it?" Angel asked.

"I think it's the end of the tunnel," Zack

called. I took a deep breath, since there seemed to be more air and it wasn't as musty smelling. The tunnel had opened into a wider space. Zack shined his flashlight to the left and the right.

"Look, there's a ladder," said Angel, pointing to one wall. Zack held up the flashlight to guide the way, and Angel started to climb up the wooden rungs. I followed behind her. The ladder led straight to the ceiling, where we found a rectangle of wood with a handle in the middle.

"It must be another trapdoor, like the one in the factory," Zack called.

"But where does it come out?" I whispered.

"Maybe in some creepy haunted house," Angel said, biting her lip.

"Or a criminal's hideout," Zack suggested. "Maybe a gang built the tunnel leading out of the marble factory. Maybe they were smugglers or something."

"And they could be waiting for us." I cringed.

"With weapons." Zack gulped.

"I still say it's the ghost of old Thadeus Loop," Angel declared.

"What should we do?" I asked.

"We could stay down here for the rest of our lives," Zack said, "or we could make our way back to the marble factory and . . ."

"And the ghost?" Angel asked. "No thanks. There's only one thing we can do," she whispered, reaching up for the handle, "so let's get it over with quick. Here goes." She began to count slowly, "One, two, three." I shut my eyes tight. She pushed on the handle and the door opened with a loud groan.

Chapter Twelve

"**O**h, no! Tootie, not again!" Those were the first words we heard after Angel lifted the trapdoor. It was such a strange thing to hear, I shook my head, thinking I must have heard wrong. I opened my eyes and saw Angel climbing through the passage above me.

"It's OK," she called down to us, "no one is here."

Zack and I followed her up the ladder. We found ourselves in a tiny, dark room. There was the faintest smell of something rotten or moldy. In the light coming through the slats of the wooden walls, I could see a large toilet seat perched on the mound behind us.

"Hurry, Mom, Tootie's in the tub again!"

"Tootie's in the tub?" Angel and I repeated. We could hear barking and the sounds of water splashing. Then we heard a lot of laughter and the sound of footsteps going by. We rushed to the door and opened it a crack. My mouth dropped open as I saw Tootie splashing around in the old bathtub in Aunt Shell's back-yard. Jack and Nelson and the Brisson boys were running out of the house in their bathing suits.

"Look," I gasped, "it's Tootie, all right. She *is* in the tub."

"Who's Tootie?" Zack asked.

"She's my aunt and uncle's dog," I told him, moving over so he could have a look through the crack. "We must be in the outhouse. That tunnel was dug from the factory to the out-house." As we listened to the boys' voices and Tootie barking, we were so relieved, we just stood there grinning. Then Zack and I leaned against the door and began to push, but Angel stopped us.

"We can't go out there yet," she said. "We've got to wait until the coast is clear."

"What are you talking about?" Zack whis-pered. Angel explained how we were forbid-den to go down to the hollow, and if we walked out of the outhouse now, everyone would ask how we got there, and the boys would tell the grown-ups.

"But don't you think we should tell them anyway?" Zack asked. "Maybe they could figure out what's going on."

Angel frowned. "If we tell them, Jenna will get in trouble with her aunt and uncle, and I'll get in really big trouble with my daddy."

If I ran out of there, I don't think I would have gotten into as much trouble as Angel, but because she was my best friend for life, I knew I couldn't leave.

"Look, Zack," I said, "we kept our end of the bargain. We came with you to the factory. Now instead of going back tonight with us, how about just keeping this whole thing a secret, so we won't get into trouble?"

"I can't even tell my brothers? Not even Ben?"

"Not even Ben," I said, shaking my head. "It's got to be a secret. You've got to swear."

"OK." Zachary nodded. "But what about your brother? I thought you wanted to get him to talk?"

"I do," I told him, "but I'll have to come up with a better plan. Going back into that hollow is too dangerous."

"I agree," Angel said. "I wonder what that old ghost would have done if he had caught us."

"I still think it could have been a gang of criminals," Zack said. "I wonder if they got a good look at us."

"I don't think so," Angel said. "We jumped off that table and found the tunnel before they even got to the basement."

"Well, you two can wonder about it all you want to," I said, closing the trapdoor. "As for me, I'm staying as far away from Marble Hollow as I can." We grew quiet as we heard Aunt Shell calling everyone into the house. I waited a few minutes and then scanned the yard. When it was empty, I pushed the old outhouse door open.

We walked out onto the grass, and I heard a noise. I spun around and found Nelson sitting in the sandpile. His left eyebrow shot up the way it always does when he's surprised, and he turned on his flashlight and pointed it in our direction.

"Oh, no," I groaned, "where did he come from?"

"At least we don't have to worry about him telling anyone that he saw us," Angel said.

She was right, but I still felt uneasy about Nelson seeing us leave the outhouse. We quickly closed the door and made our way to the sandpile.

"It's a good thing that trapdoor wasn't locked, or we'd still be stuck down in that tunnel," Zack said. I looked over at Nelson whose eyebrows shot up even more. I grabbed Zack's arm and pulled him aside.

"Why did you say that in front of Nelson?" I demanded.

"What's the difference?" Zack complained. "He can't talk. He won't tell anyone." I could feel my cheeks flush with anger.

"He may not be able to talk, but he can hear, and he's not dumb," I whispered. "He understands everything you say. He's not a dummy, you know."

"I'm really sorry, Jenna," Zack apologized. "I guess that was *dumb* of me." He looked truly sorry, but I still felt bad.

Just then Aunt Shell came out looking for Nelson. I reached down and picked up an empty plastic berry-picking bucket from the sandpile. Aunt Shell must have thought we had eaten all the berries we had gone to pick.

She pretended to scold us, but you could tell she wasn't really mad.

Ben and Noah dragged Zack off to look at an old snakeskin they had found by the shed. Aunt Shell fixed us some crackers and cheese, and we sat at the kitchen table trying to make conversation with her and Mrs. Brisson. It wasn't easy, since we were still shaken up over everything that had happened.

"Are you feeling all right?" Aunt Shell asked, putting her hand on my forehead.

"I'm OK," I told her. "I'm just a little tired."

"That's what you get for staying up and talking last night," she said. "Why don't you take a nap?"

I hadn't taken a nap since the first grade, but it seemed like a good way to get out of the kitchen, so Angel and I agreed. We walked to the porch and I flopped down on the cot. Angel looked through the screen toward the barn where the Brisson boys were playing.

"What are you looking at?" I asked.

"Just stuff," she said, sitting down beside me.

"I don't think I'll ever get that hollow out of

my mind," I whispered, staring up at the porch ceiling.

"We got away by the skin of our teeth, you know that, Jenna Pearl?"

"I know," I said. "We were really lucky that the tunnel ended up where it did."

"Why would someone build a tunnel from the factory to an outhouse?" Angel mused. "Unless they had something to hide."

"I think I'll have nightmares about that old walking stick coming though that window for the rest of my life," I whispered.

"I can call home and ask if I can stay over again. Then you won't have to sleep alone," Angel offered.

I smiled and sat up. "I don't think I'll ever have a better best friend than you," I told her.

"Same goes for me," she replied. "It's funny how you can have all kinds of friends. Then one day you meet someone who means more to you than all the rest. Someone you can tell your darkest secrets to, someone who would loan you their best clothes." She paused here, and neither of us said anything. Finally I asked, "Do you want to borrow any of my clothes?"

"No, silly." She laughed. "I was just tryin' to tell you how I feel." Her face turned serious, her voice low and whispery. "But I do have a secret."

I nodded, waiting.

"You understand this is a secret between you and me and no other livin' soul?"

"No one else," I promised.

"On your honor, you won't tell anyone? And you hope to die a horrible long and painful death, if you do?" she insisted.

"On my honor. Now will you go ahead and tell me?" I pleaded.

"Last week, when Shana met Cole . . ."

"Shana who?" I interrupted.

"You know, the girl I was telling you about on 'One Bright World,'" Angel explained. "The one who had been really ugly and had had no boyfriends, until she was in the car accident and had to have plastic surgery, which turned her into the most gorgeous girl in Brently Heights, and then suddenly all the men wanted to go out with her."

"Not another soap." I groaned, but this didn't stop Angel.

"Well, last week Cole, who is this really

handsome architect with lots of money and a dimple in his chin, moved to Brently Heights. Anyway, Shana was sitting across from Cole at this dinner party, and their eyes sort of locked, you know how that happens when two people fall instantly in love. And Shana went home and wrote in her diary that her life had been transformed, because she had met her soul mate, the man she knew she would someday marry. . . ."

"So if it was on TV, how's it a secret?" I asked.

"The secret's not about them." Angel sighed. "It's about me. Look at these," she said, holding out her arm. I looked down to see a wave of little bumps covering her arm.

"Those are the good kind of goose bumps," she said.

"But how? Why?"

"I guess it's just from thinkin' about him." She smiled.

"Him, who? Angel, what are you talking about?"

"Jenna Pearl, don't you see? My life has been transformed. I have met my soul mate. The man I will someday marry."

"You have?" I gasped. "What man?"

"Well, he's not a man yet, but he's gonna be one day."

"Wait a minute," I cried, "you aren't talking about Zack, are you? He's not the soul mate you're talking about, is he?"

"Why is that so surprisin'?" She sniffed.

"I don't know, it just is," I sputtered. "I knew you liked him, but to call him . . ."

"Cute, I'd call him real cute," she said.

"Cute enough to want to marry?"

"Uh-huh, I'd say so." She grinned.

"But how do you know? How can you be so sure?"

"Because it doesn't happen every day, that's how I know," Angel declared. "It's the most wonderful feelin', because you don't even have to think about it. It's just the way it is, like being struck with this rush of love. Your brain clicks off and your heart turns on. It's just like what happened between you and me. How we knew instantly that we were meant to be best friends for life, and without even thinkin' it over, we were!"

"But what about Zack?" I asked. "Do you think he's struck by 'this rush of love,' too?"

Angel made a face and looked back out through the screen. "He don't appear to be," she mumbled.

"But if he isn't struck, then how could you still like him?" I asked.

"It's plain you don't watch enough TV," she said, shaking her head. "That's what soaps are all about, Jenna Pearl. 'Cause more times than not, feelings of love don't strike two people at the very same time in the very same way. Now you take Shana, her heart was flooded with love till it was ready to burst, but Cole, he was a different story. He thought she was cute and all, but he still had his mind on his old girl-friend, Samantha, who had just married his best friend, Eric."

"It sounds awfully complicated to me," I said. "I'm glad I haven't been struck."

"It is kind of complicated," Angel agreed. "But I wouldn't trade the feelin' for anythin' in the world. It's that wonderful."

"Doesn't it hurt not to be loved back?" I asked.

"Well, of course it does. All you have to do is turn on 'One Bright World' any day of the week and you're sure to find someone cryin' their eyes out. But I think as bad as it feels, it can feel good, too. It's a powerful wonderful feelin'."

She had a dreamy look on her face as she lay back on her pillow.

The voices of the Brisson boys drifted over from the barn, but we didn't get up to look. We were too busy trading secrets and whispering about how wonderful the power of love can be. With a warm breeze sweeping in through the screens, and the buzzing of honey bees in the crabapple tree just outside the porch, it wasn't long before we were lulled to sleep.

We slept for over an hour, and then spent the rest of the day picking wildflowers to press into Aunt Shell's big dictionary. Angel, of course, looked for flowers growing by the barn, where Zack and his brothers were playing in the hayloft.

After we had all the flowers we wanted, Angel went into the house to call her mother. While she was gone, I tried to get Zack alone, so we could talk about the hollow, but his brothers kept interfering. I looked at him closely, checking for any signs of his being struck with love, but I didn't see any.

When Angel came out of the house frown-ing, I knew it was bad news.

"I have to sleep over at my granny's place tonight," she said glumly. "My folks are going bowling with my aunt and uncle, and I have to help Granny sit for my little cousin Matty."

I asked Aunt Shell if I could walk Angel partway. She agreed and asked me to stop at Peachy's for some milk. After saying good-bye to Zack, we started down the driveway. We were walking alongside the cornfield, when I noticed something shiny in the weeds.

"Oh, no," Angel gasped as I bent down to see what it was, "not another one."

I held the shimmering marble up to the sun-light. "It's exactly like the ones we found in the nest," I whispered.

"This is creepy," Angel said. "It reminds me of those two little kids in that fairy tale who left a trail of bread crumbs as they walked to the old witch's house, except in our case someone is leaving us a trail, a trail of marbles."

"Yeah," I whispered. "But I want to know *who* is the someone." I put the marble back in the grass, and we continued on our way. Angel didn't seem as chatty as usual, and we were both quiet. Finding that marble had brought back the whole terrifying experience of the hollow, and with all of it, our unanswered questions.

When we came to the fork in the road, we reached out and gave each other a hug. Then we stood still. Neither of us wanted to walk the rest of the way alone. Even though it was broad daylight and we were nowhere near the old marble factory, it was hard to shake the fear that had gripped us in the hollow.

"I'll call you later," Angel promised as we hugged again. I walked the rest of the way to Peachy's, wondering about everything that had happened. My mind was so preoccupied that I walked up to Peachy's door in a daze. I put my hand on the metal door handle, and Jasper jumped off the bench to my right. My eyes focused, and I let out a shriek. Leaning against the bench was the walking stick. The same snake curved around it with the green shimmering marble in its mouth. The very same walking stick that I was certain to have nightmares about for the rest of my life!

Chapter Thirteen

"Jasper won't hurt ya. The mice aren't even afraid of him anymore," a voice boomed from behind me. I spun around. A heavyset man with a blotchy red face and a big bumpy nose was standing a few feet away. I almost cried out with relief when I saw his blue hat and uniform.

"Are . . . are . . . you a policeman?" I stammered.

"Sounds like a trick question to me, Kenny," another voice called from inside the screen door.

"You shut your face up, Dewy Miller," the policeman shouted into the store. He looked back at me. I realized he wanted me to open the door. Before I knew what was happening, I pulled on the handle and stepped inside. A wave of cold air blasted me from Peachy's old air conditioner. Another policeman, a much smaller man with bushy blond hair, was standing at the checkout counter paying Peachy for a sandwich. The policeman called Kenny walked over to the air conditioner.

"Hey, Peachy, what are ya tryin' to do with this old thing, give us all frostbite?" he joked. Peachy walked over to the air conditioner and banged on it with his fist.

"Darn thing is stuck on High," he complained. The three men took turns trying to get the High knob to move. The sound of their voices was so reassuring, it gave me the courage to look down the first aisle. It was empty. I walked to the next aisle and stood in front of some cat food bags, craning my neck to see around the corner. It was empty, too. There was only one aisle left in the store. I thought about running away and maybe catching up with Angel, but then I heard the cough.

It was coming from the last aisle. It sounded like an old cough from old lungs. My hands began to sweat as I picked up a box of cereal and put it back down. I was certain that the owner of those old lungs was also the owner of the walking stick. What would a ghost be doing out in broad daylight, if that's what it was? I tried to force myself to take a step down the aisle, but I couldn't. I was too petrified.

At least the police are here, I reminded myself. I turned to look for them, but they had given up on the air conditioner and gone over to the far wall by the toilet paper. They were busy staring up at their turkey trophies.

"Best beard in Mifflin County," one of them said. They might be talking about turkeys, I thought, but at least if I screamed they'd be close enough to hear me. As I listened to the creak of a cart's wheels in the other aisle, I was sure I would scream any moment.

Peachy must have noticed how I wasn't moving. He tilted his head and gave me a long stare. I looked back, trying to smile as I fingered a bag of cat food.

"What'ya lookin' fer?" he asked.

"M . . . mi . . . milk," I squeaked.

"Ain't going to find it with the cat food," he said.

"No, I guess not," I mumbled. I took a small step toward the cooler. Just as I did, an old man and woman came around the corner. They took no notice of me as my hand reached for a bottle of dish soap. I was squeezing it so hard, I was afraid the top would pop open and the soap would come squirting out.

I watched, wide-eyed, as the old man came limping down the aisle behind one of Peachy's little carts. He had no hair on his shiny bald head, although I noticed some gray tufts coming out of his ears and some spiky whiskers on his chin. He was wearing faded blue overalls that were so short, you could see his bony ankles sticking out above his wrinkly, stained socks and cracked leather shoes. On either side of his beaklike nose were watery blue eyes, rimmed with dark circles.

Walking beside him was a withered old woman in a green dress with big black buttons. She had the same beak nose, but her sunken eyes were smaller and brighter. Her skin was waxy with wrinkles and her silver hair shot out from her head in straggly wisps.

My eyes dropped to the old woman's hands. My heart raced as her long, gnarled, yellowed fingers reached for a box of cereal on the lower shelf. I was sure those were the same gnarly fingers Angel had seen. The woman's thin arms were covered in goose bumps.

It wasn't a ghost, I was thinking. Zack's

right. Ghosts don't get goose bumps. So maybe she's a witch! A witch could get goose bumps. Then before I could take another step, the old man began throwing cans of tomato sauce into the cart.

"Now don't you go startin' up, Win," the woman scolded in a creaky voice. She slapped his hand as if he were a child, and I realized that as old as he looked, there was also something childlike about him. Part of it was his clothes, which seemed to be too small, but it was also the look on his face. His eyes were wide-open, like a baby's, and he had a pout that reminded me of Jack's when he was crabby and needed a nap.

"Maybe he's tryin' to tell you somethin', Miss Neva," Peachy said, coming down the aisle. He took a can of tomato sauce away from the old man.

"You feelin' like havin' some of those Spa-ghettiOs tonight? Is that what it is?" Peachy asked. But the old man just broke into giggles and looked away.

"He don't care what he eats," the old woman said. "Likely as not, he'd eat that cat food there, if I let him."

I walked over to the cooler as quietly as I could and looked in at the cartons of milk. Every now and then I stole a glance to my right, watching as the old couple made their way to the counter. By the time they had checked out, Kenny and Dewy had grown tired of talking about turkey feet and had returned to the front of the store.

Kenny offered to hold open the door for the old woman and the old man with his cart full of bags. The screen door slammed shut behind them. I stood for a while longer looking into the cooler, then reached for a carton of milk.

"She sure has got her plate full, that Miss Neva," Kenny remarked, looking out the screen door, "what with that old boy."

"Loony Loop de Loop," Dewy said with a chuckle.

"Ever since the accident, things have been going downhill for that family," Peachy said. "First his leg went bad, then his mind. He was good up to a few years ago. Shame what some folks have to endure."

"My granddaddy's still got some of those marbles from the factory when it first opened up," Dewy remarked.

"Expect most folks around here do," Peachy replied.

"Shame she had to lose the place to them Northeast Industries people," Kenny said.

"They'd been after her for years to sell her land." Peachy sighed. "But Miss Neva could never part with her daddy's factory. Said she'd as like to part with one of her limbs. Then after things started goin' bad and her money all run out, she was forced to let it go. They swindled her, of course, like all those fat cats do. If she had gotten the fair price, she'd be a rich woman right now. Heard her tell my aunt Mattie she'd like to throw a hex on the whole lot of them."

"Fer starters, she could get herself a new car," Kenny said. "That sorry old truck she drives looks old as dirt."

I handed Peachy my money, and he handed back my change. Reluctantly I picked up my milk carton and headed for the door, walking as slowly as I could. I wanted to hear more abut this "hex" business, but Dewy had sidetracked the conversation to turkey feet.

"Talkin' about the holler, do you remember that bird I brought down last spring? Now wouldn't you say it was twice as big as . . ."

I pushed open the screen door. The late afternoon sun was like a huge golden red ball coming down behind the ridge. A line of evergreen trees stood shimmering in the glow of the smoldering orange light. And on the road, heading straight into that fiery scene, was a worn yellow pickup truck with old Neva Loop at the wheel.

Chapter Fourteen

I raced back to the farm, having to stop twice when I dropped the carton of milk. Luckily it didn't break open. I reached the yard and waved to Aunt Shell and Mrs. Brisson, who were busy pulling clothes from the clothesline. I was glad to find the kitchen empty so I could call Angel. I put the milk in the refrigerator and dialed her number.

"Are you sure it was the same walking stick?" she asked, after I explained about seeing the Loops at Peachy's.

"I'm positive," I said. "It was the same dark wood with the snake carved all around it, and the green marble in its mouth."

Angel insisted I give her "the complete story, just as it happened," so I repeated all I could remember.

"What do you think?" I asked.

"I'm not sure," she said. "Did Peachy mention anything about a tunnel?"

"No," I told her.

"There could still be a ghost," Angel whispered. "The ghost of old Thadeus Loop, or old Miss Neva could be a witch."

"Or Zack could be right, maybe they're smugglers," I suggested.

"But if they were smugglers, they'd be driving around in fancy cars and livin' in a fancy house, unless . . ."

"Unless they are trying to hide their wealth," I said. We talked for a little longer, but Angel had to get off the phone, since her brother Ricky wanted to call his girlfriend.

Angel promised to call me later from her grandmother's, and we hung up. I went out to the porch steps and sat down, staring at the old blue outhouse. What was the tunnel for? I wondered. What were those old Loops doing making marbles in the middle of the night? And what would have happened to us if they had caught us? There were so many unanswered questions about that hollow, so many strange things going on. In my mind I followed the creek as it wove its way through the woods, out past the old factory sitting in the weeds.

Suddenly I was feeling homesick, homesick for my mother and father, who usually could answer most of my questions. And homesick for the straight lines of Summit, for all the straight streets and sidewalks lit with streetlights and the comforting glow of houses and stores everywhere. Things were normal there, I was thinking. There were no surprises, no grizzly bears.

I went back into the kitchen and dialed my home number. I knew I couldn't tell my parents about what had happened, but I needed to hear their voices. The phone rang and rang, but no one was home.

As I hung up the phone, Aunt Shell came into the kitchen. Mrs. Brisson was behind her.

"Where's Nelson?" she asked. "Did he go upstairs?"

"No, I didn't see him," I told her.

"But wasn't he with you when you walked Angel home?"

"No," I said, shaking my head. "Angel and I went alone. Haven't you seen him since then?"

"Come to think of it, I haven't," she answered. "With all the kids rushing in and out, it's hard to keep track of everybody." She turned to Mrs. Brisson. "Pat, have you seen Nelson this afternoon?"

"No, but maybe he's with the guys. Hold on, I'll go see." I wasn't too worried, since Nelson, being silent, is often missed, even when he's in the very same room with people. Mrs. Brisson came back with Zachary and Jack. The other Brisson boys straggled up from the barn, sweaty and flushed from having raced each other around the old sheds. But Nelson wasn't with them.

We finally figured out that the last time anyone had seen him was just before Angel and I started down the driveway. That was more than an hour ago. We searched the house first, and when we didn't find him, we began to search outside. The Brisson boys fanned out around the barn, Aunt Shell and Mrs. Brisson looked in the garden, and Jack and I walked along the fields. Everyone was calling Nelson's name. I expected his head of dark hair to pop up suddenly, but it never did.

Uncle Mark and Mr. Brisson were in one of the sheds working on an old manure spreader.

They put down their tools and joined in the search, calling for Nelson in their deep, throaty voices. The sun was going down behind the cornfield, and the sky was filling up with big dark clouds. I could see the worry in Aunt Shell's eyes and the wrinkles forming on Uncle Mark's forehead. The sound of thunder echoed over the ridge, and the pine trees trembled as a sudden gust of wind blew up.

"Look's like a storm coming on," I heard Uncle Mark whisper to my aunt. I bit down on my lip, trying not to cry. Mrs. Brisson took Jack and the younger boys back to the house so "they won't go getting lost, too."

"I don't understand it," Aunt Shell said. "He was afraid of the woods, so I know he wouldn't go walking off alone."

"Well, we've checked the barn," Uncle Mark said. "And the house and the sheds. How about the outhouse? Did anyone check there?"

My stomach knotted up so much that I let out a little groan. "I'll look," I stammered.

"I'll go with you," offered Zack.

"Good, and try the cornfield after that," Aunt Shell suggested. "The corn's tall enough that he may have lost his way."

"While you two do that, we'll try the barn again," said Uncle Mark. I took off for the outhouse, my heart pounding in my ears. Zack ran beside me.

"Why did I leave Nelson alone after we came out of there? I was so stupid!" I blurted when we were out of earshot.

"You don't even know he went in there, Jenna," Zack replied. "And if he did, maybe he didn't use the trapdoor. Maybe he fell asleep. Little kids take naps all the time. I'll bet we'll find him sound asleep."

"Could you fall asleep in an outhouse?" I moaned. As I grabbed the door handle, I shut my eyes and imagined Nelson curled up asleep in front of the old toilet seat.

"Please let him be there, please," I whispered under my breath as I pulled the door open.

"Oh, no!" Zack gasped. We stood staring down at the trapdoor. It was wide open. "It's all my fault!" Zack cried. "It's all my fault!"

Chapter Fifteen

Zack's wrong. It's all *my* fault, I thought as I stared into the dark tunnel. If I hadn't gone to the hollow in the first place, none of this would be happening now.

"Nelson, Nelson. Where are you, Nelson?" The frantic voices of my aunt, uncle, and Mr. Brisson drifted out of the hayloft, followed by a boom of thunder in the distance.

"They can call him until they're blue in the face," I whispered, stepping into the out-house, "but he won't be able to hear them, not if he's down in the tunnel. I've got to find him."

"Jenna, wait," Zack said. "You can't go back there again, not after what happened last time."

"I can't not go back," I answered. "Nelson's

gone down there. And I've got to get him out."

"Shouldn't we tell your aunt and uncle first?"

"You know I can't. I promised Angel not to tell, and you did, too," I reminded him.

Zack followed me into the outhouse, then reached over and pulled the door shut.

"If we're going to keep this a secret," he said, "we can't have this door wide open."

"But . . . you . . . you're going with me?" I stammered.

"Well, how do you expect to find your way without this?" Zack asked, pulling his little flashlight out of his back pocket. "Besides, I was the one who shot off my mouth in front of Nelson, mentioning the trapdoor the way I did. The least I can do is help you find him."

"Angel was right." I grinned. "You really do have distinction."

"Huh?" Zack made a face and started down the rungs of the ladder. I followed close behind. When we jumped off the last rung, I was disappointed not to find Nelson waiting at the bottom.

"He must have gone through," Zack said. He shined his flashlight into the dark tunnel.

"Nelson," I called, poking my head into the blackness. "Don't worry, Nelson, we're coming." But there was no reply. I didn't really expect an answer, but I craned my neck, straining to hear any sound, any evidence, that he was there. The stillness was deadly.

"It's a good thing he carries that flashlight with him wherever he goes," Zack said as he made his way through the passageway in front of me.

"Even with his light, he's all alone," I said, my eyes filling with tears. "Hurry, Zack, hurry," I pleaded. We began to run through the tunnel, but my hopes of finding Nelson there grew slimmer and slimmer. There was no light ahead from his flashlight, and no sound of his feet running to meet us. I kept imagining him in the clutches of that old witch, Neva Loop, and her crazy brother. Would they beat him with their walking stick? Would they cast a spell on him? What if he fell into the furnace? What if he were pushed? I shook my head, trying to get rid of the frightening pictures that were flashing across my mind.

"What are you stopping for?" I yelled as Zack slumped down against a wall.

"I have to catch my breath for a minute," he gasped. I pushed the flashlight up to his face and in the little glow of light, I could see that his cheeks had become very red. His chest was heaving up and down and his breathing was growing heavier and heavier.

"Your inhaler, use your inhaler," I cried.

"I . . . can't," he wheezed. "I gave it to Angel to look at and I forgot to get it back. I'll be OK, I just need to rest."

I knelt down beside him and put my arm on his shoulder. "We must be halfway there," I said, trying to keep the nervousness out of my voice. "We needed to take a rest anyway." He didn't answer, except to nod. I thought if we talked, it would take his mind off things and help him to calm down. Since he needed to save his breath, I was the one who did all the talking. I talked about Nelson, because he was all that was on my mind.

"Nelson's afraid of the dark, you know," I began. "That's why he carries that flashlight wherever he goes. I hope the batteries don't go dead. Even when he was a baby, he always needed a little light on."

Zack gave out a small grunt. "Like my

brother Gabriel," he gasped. "He's always . . ." But Zack's sentence sputtered off into a series of wheezes, and as I listened to his labored breathing, I realized that he wasn't getting better. I thought about that girl who had died of asthma last year at the high school. I started wondering what she sounded like before she died.

A panicky feeling swept over me as I tried to figure out what to do next. How was Zack going to make it back to the farm and his inhaler? How was Nelson going to be saved, since we were the only ones who knew where he was? Zack couldn't go anywhere, not now anyway. Maybe if he rested and got his breath, I could help him back to the farm. But I didn't have time to wait. If I was going to save Nelson from whatever evil lurked in that old marble factory, I had to do it now and that meant doing it alone.

"Zack, listen to me," I said, reaching for his arm, "I have to go and get Nelson. You wait here and rest, and I'll come back for you as soon as I can. Will you be OK till I get back?"

His face was flushed a beet red by now, and it was hard for him to talk.

"Take . . . take . . . this," he gasped, shoving the flashlight in my hand.

"No," I said, pushing it back, "you keep it, and if you feel like you're getting worse, try and make it to the outhouse without me." I squeezed his hand. It was cold and clammy and we were both trembling. As I started off into the darkness, I could hear him sucking in great gulps of air, then came long whistling wheezes. The sounds were growing fainter and fainter, and the last thing I heard was his weakened voice straining painfully to be heard.

"I'll wait for you, Jenna. I won't go back without you."

It was comforting to hear him say that, but not for long, since the true danger of my situation was dawning on me. Zack could die in this tomblike tunnel. Nelson could meet with a worse fate at the hands of some old witch putting a hex on him. And me? What was going to happen to me?

Chapter Sixteen

I've never been a very brave person, certainly not as brave as Angel or Zack. I groped my way along the cold, damp sides of the tunnel and thought about how I hated the dark as much as Nelson did.

If only he hadn't seen us leaving the outhouse, I thought. I should have warned him not to go in there. Why hadn't I done that? If only I had been a better sister. I knew deep down in my heart that there were times I had been ashamed of Nelson and his being unable to talk. These guilty thoughts nagged at me now. I had never told anyone about these bad feelings, not even Angel. I was ashamed to admit how embarrassed he made me feel and how I had even been relieved to hear that Nelson would be going to a different school. I didn't want my school friends to see him.

And now the tears were running down my cheeks at the thought that *I* might never see him again! I found myself talking out loud, just to keep from crying.

"I wish you were here with me now, Angel." My shaky voice echoed off the tunnel's walls. "I wish I had your glasses to help me see better, and I wish I had your courage. I wish I wasn't afraid of rats and spiderwebs and . . ." My voice trailed off as I rounded a bend and found myself facing the door to the factory's cellar.

OK, this is it, I thought to myself. Please let him be here. Oh, please let him be here. I took a deep breath and opened the door. It was so dark that I bumped into a barrel. I stood frozen to the spot, my ears straining to hear the slightest sound or movement.

"Nelson," I whispered, my voice cracking with fear, "Nelson, are you in here?" I stumbled around the room, my arms outstretched, feeling my way, hoping to find him, but he wasn't there. I finally reached the stone steps that led up to the factory. I had stopped thinking about what I was doing. I was more like a robot operating on automatic. I was going to find Nelson no matter what I had to do and where I had to go. When I reached the top step, I felt around with my arms over my head, and found the trapdoor. I tried pushing it open, but it wouldn't budge. Someone must have locked it, I decided.

That's when it occurred to me that maybe Nelson hadn't gone down the tunnel after all. Maybe he had just opened the trapdoor in the outhouse and then gone off to play somewhere else on the farm. If that were so, I could run back to Zack and we could end this nightmare right now.

A wave of relief washed over me, and I smiled at the thought of Nelson asleep in the cornfield, or behind one of the sheds, somewhere safe and far from the clutches of the Loops and their haunted marble factory. Yes, I decided, he's definitely not here.

I was making my way back down the other side of the steps when I tripped. It wasn't anything big that made me stumble, like a barrel or crate, but rather something small. I shrieked in terror, imagining a mouse or a rat. As I listened to the object roll and hit each step, I calmed down, since it didn't sound like an animal. Carefully making my way down the

stairs, I felt around with my foot, nudging something with my sneaker. It was definitely not a rat. It rolled like a bottle or a can. I bent down and with trembling fingers picked it up.

I knew what it was the minute I had it in my hands. My heart sank as my fingers traveled over the familiar shape. I shuddered as I flicked on the switch, sending a bright beam of light out into the darkness. It was Nelson's flashlight, all right, but where was Nelson?

Chapter Seventeen

I directed the flashlight into every corner of the room, but all I saw were crates and barrels and spiders dangling from their webs. I climbed the steps again and put my ear to the trapdoor. A cold shiver ran down my back as I heard footsteps overhead and the sharp knock of something hitting the floor.

"The walking stick!" I sputtered. My knees knocked together as I stood listening. Suddenly the trapdoor was flung open, and I was staring up at the shriveled old figure of Neva Loop herself!

"Aghh!" I screamed, shutting my eyes tight. Too terrified to move, I cracked open an eye and caught sight of Nelson's two little green sneakers swinging off a table. In his hand was the walking stick. I almost fell backward with relief.

"Nelson!" I cried, forgetting my fear and rushing up the top steps, past the old woman. "Are you all right?" I threw my arms around him, almost knocking over the lantern on the table next to him. He grinned, tapping the floor once more with the stick.

"He's fit as can be, ain't ya, honey?" old Miss Loop said. I gripped Nelson's arm at the sound of her creaky voice, all my fears rushing back. The old man was standing beside her, a strange smile on his face. I held my breath as he walked toward us. Without saying a word, he stretched his hand toward Nelson. Nelson handed Irwin Loop the walking stick. I slumped against the table with relief as the old man slowly made his way across the room, using the strange stick to lean on.

"But he shouldn't ought to be playin' down the tunnel, and neither should you," Miss Loop said. "This ain't no place for little ones to be playin'." She sat down on a dusty chair and picked up a ball of yarn and some knitting needles from a plastic bag on the floor. "I reckon you both had a bad scare today, so jes' you stay put and rest up a bit, now."

I didn't budge, except to look at Nelson,

who didn't seem frightened at all. Meanwhile old Miss Loop began to hum softly as she looped the yarn over her needles. My eyes followed her gaze as she turned to look at the other end of the room, where her brother was busy stoking the furnace. There were a number of lanterns lit, and the smell of kerosene tickled my nose. As frightened as I was, I felt a twinge of relief at seeing the old man at the furnace. At least he's not a ghost, I thought.

"I told Irwin to board up that trapdoor years ago," Miss Loop said, "but he never paid me no mind. You see, he loves this place, it being built by our granddaddy and all. Still can't keep away, after all these years."

The longer I listened, the better her voice sounded. It was old and creaky but calm, not excited or shrieky like I imagined a witch's would be.

"Are you . . . are you smugglers?" I croaked.

"Smugglers?" Miss Loop cocked her head as if she hadn't heard right.

"Is that why you built the tunnel?" I squeaked. "To use for smuggling?"

The old woman let out a cackle of laughter.

"Mercy me, girl, you have some imagination! Why, that tunnel's been there since before the war. That would be the Civil War. You see, my family were pledged to the Union and freedom. They were what was known as abolitionists. The tunnel was used to transfer colored folk from slavery to freedom. They would come from all over the South, Georgia and Alabama, making their way up north. This was one of the last stops on the route."

I had studied the Civil War in school last year, and I knew about the abolitionists and their tunnels. The journey the slaves made, stopping in secret at white peoples' houses, was called the Underground Railroad. So the Loops weren't smugglers, and it wasn't a ghost making the marbles. That left only one other possibility. Witchcraft. Looking at the walking stick that the old man had laid against a table, I couldn't help but wonder.

"What about the walking stick? Is it magical or something?" My voice was still shaky.

Miss Loop smiled. "Only to me and Irwin," she said softly. "You see, it belonged to our daddy. He had it carved in Europe. It's a one of a kind, I reckon, a real treasure. When he was in his heyday, with the factory doing well and the money comin' in, we had such things. Oh, I wish you could have seen the fine things. Did you see the beautiful marble in the snake's mouth?" I nodded. But there was something still nagging at me.

"About the marbles, why are you making them at night?" I asked.

"That's Irwin's need to keep workin' in the old place," the old woman explained. "Now, some folks might not approve, seein' how it's not legally our factory anymore, but I know how Irwin feels. He worked his whole life makin' them marbles, and it's the only work he knows."

"But what about the people that bought the factory?" I asked.

Miss Loop put down her needles and frowned. "That would be Northeast Industries. They tore up the land as far over as Lightnin' Ridge. Turns out they didn't even want this holler. Last I heard they had it up for sale at twice the price they paid me. 'Course I had no money left by then. If it hadn't been for Win's going off crazy and havin' to close the factory, they'd never been able to set foot on our land. Didn't pay enough to last us more than a year or so."

"You mean your brother sneaks back here to make the marbles, and they don't know he's here?" I asked.

"They send a man from the company over now and then to check on things. Lucky thing is he don't come at night." Miss Loop took up her needles and yarn again. "Irwin's as gentle as a baby. Jest loves makin' marbles, is all. And he's darn good at it, too. So till they tear the place down, or sell it off, I don't see the harm in his havin' his way."

"And do you always come with him?" I asked. She smiled, turning to look at the old man.

"Who else would? Most of our kin have died or moved away, and the others, the young people, see nothin' but the crazy side of him now. It's true he's not of right mind, but they don't know the Irwin I know. They don't see his goodness the way I do. I suppose that's because I'm his sister. I can see past the fits and spells."

I nodded.

"I'm all he's got left to look after him now,"

she continued, "and though he goes gettin' me mad every now and then with his stubborn ways, he ain't no bother, really. He's happy to come down here to work, and I always bring my needlework to keep me occupied," she said, picking up her yarn. "That's how we came by findin' you two. I had forgot my needlework, and we stopped by in the afternoon so I could pick it up. When Win saw the broken window, he poked his stick in. I thought I heard a scream and figured some kids must've got into the place, and so we opened the door and looked around. Then Win and I went to town to get a new pane for the window. After he fixed the window, Win got to fiddlin' with the machines and so I jes' sat and worked on my knittin', 'stead of goin' on home again. Win's got a natural 'bility with machines, don't you know."

As I watched her wrinkled fingers bend around the knitting needles, I thought about what she had said. I began to see that her love for her brother was a lot like my love for Nelson. Her smile suddenly faded.

"Don't expect to have him with me much longer, though, with our moneys all runnin' out."

"Why don't you sell the marbles he makes now?" I suggested.

Miss Loop shook her head. "I expect we could get into some trouble jest for being here. No, Win's marbles go right down to the cellar, 'cepting the ones I bring home to display. He loves to put them out around the place and to hide them so people are surprised when they come upon them. I've found them in the strangest places."

"Like birds' nests?" I asked.

Miss Loop laughed. "Why, yes, even there. I suppose Irwin sometimes likes to surprise the birds. If I could have a dollar for every marble I've come across in an unexpected place, I'd be rich right now, instead of skimmin' bottom."

"What will you do if you run out of money?" I asked.

Miss Loop turned to look back at her brother. "Expect he'll need to go to the state hospital over in Mifflinsburg, 'cause I can't look after him no more and I can't afford a nurse."

There was so much sadness in her voice, I felt guilty for having thought she was a witch. I knew how she must feel about her brother, and I snuggled closer to Nelson on the table.

Miss Loop was about to say something else, but a loud crash echoed up from the cellar. That's when I remembered Zack!

"Irwin, go see what it is," Miss Loop ordered. The old man slowly made his way across the room.

"Zack!" I cried, jumping off the table. I went rushing to the trapdoor. Miss Loop held a lantern as we went down the steps. I found Zack gasping beside an overturned barrel. There were marbles rolling everywhere, but Zack took no notice. His eyes were half closed, and he was trying to talk.

"Don't," I told him, "don't try to say anything. Save your breath. You should have gone back to the outhouse. You should have gone back to the farm."

He tried to answer, but couldn't. I wiped away the spit that was coming out of his mouth. "It's OK. Everything is OK. Look who's here. It's Nelson. He's safe." Nelson peeked out from behind me. A faint smile crept onto Zack's face before his eyes began to close, and he was overcome with another fit of wheezing.

I explained Zack's asthma to Miss Loop, and how he had risked his life to come help me find Nelson.

"He needs to get to a hospital," Miss Loop said. "His breath's not comin' right.

"Irwin, pick the child up and carry him to the truck," she ordered. The old man handed his walking stick to Nelson. Then he stooped over and gently took Zack in his arms. It scared me to see how limp Zack was. His arms dangled down and his face had gone from red to chalky white. And why wasn't he opening his eyes?

Please don't die, Zack. Please don't die, I prayed as hard as I could, following them up the cellar steps. That's when I first smelled smoke.

Chapter Eighteen

By the time we reached the top stair, the smoke was swirling around us. My eyes darted to a small fire that was overtaking a table not far from the furnace's open door.

"The furnace!" Miss Loop cried. "Irwin, you forgot to shut the door!" The old man started across the smoke-filled room, with Zack still in his arms.

"No, it's too late now," Miss Loop yelled. "We've got to get the children out of here! Hurry, Win. Hurry!" She grabbed hold of Nelson's left hand, and I took his right. Together we three hurried across the room toward the door. Irwin couldn't move as fast with his bad leg, and the smoke seemed to be overcoming him. When we reached the middle of the room, I turned and saw him fall, with Zack still cradled in his arms. I wanted to go back for them, but Miss Loop was tugging Nelson away. As we headed for the door, a ceiling beam came crashing down, blocking our way.

"The window!" I yelled to Miss Loop. "If we can make it to the window, we can get out that way." My eyes were tearing so badly that it was hard to see. That's when I felt Nelson's hand pull away from mine.

"Nelson!" I screamed, reaching my arms out into the dense smoke, hoping to grab him. But it was as if he and old Miss Neva had vanished. Another ceiling beam came crashing down in front of me, and I jumped out of the way. I felt a hand grab my arm, and for an instant I thought it was Nelson, but when I spun around, I saw that it was Irwin Loop, with Zack in his arms. The old man began pulling me toward the window.

"No," I screamed, trying to pull away, "I can't leave my brother. My brother's somewhere in here!" That's the last thing I remember before everything went black.

When I came to, the first thing I felt was a wave of cool air wash over my face. Then I realized I was being carried in someone's arms. My eyes were still closed and my head was spinning. I heard a lot of voices around me. Then I felt a little hand press into mine and I opened my eyes to see Nelson's smudged face beside mine.

I reached out to hug him, and suddenly Uncle Mark and Aunt Shell were there and everyone was hugging and crying together. A person from the rescue squad was checking my pulse and my heartbeat, and when they were certain I was OK, they tapped me on the head and told me to "lay low for a while." But I couldn't sit still.

"What about Zack?" I cried, sitting up. "And the Loops? Are they all right?"

"They all got out, and everyone is safe," Aunt Shell said quickly. She pointed to Zack and the Loops who were surrounded by the rescue squad.

"But how?" I mumbled.

"Miss Loop and Nelson got out through the door," Uncle Mark explained. "The old woman was in a state of shock and didn't know where she was. The firemen were going to go back in that way for the rest of you, but Nelson told them to go to the window."

"Nelson?" I croaked. "What do you mean, 'Nelson told them'?"

"Go ahead, Nelson, why don't you show her how you did it," Uncle Mark said, placing his hand on Nelson's shoulder. I turned and watched Nelson's tearstained face break into a grin. He sucked in a mouthful of air, then let it out. Suddenly all the noise around us stopped, and all I could hear was this one little voice.

"The window, Jenna's at the window." Although it was a voice I had never heard before, I recognized it instantly. It was my brother's voice. It was Nelson talking!

"But . . . but . . . how?" I stammered as I pulled him to me, crying and laughing at once. "How did this happen?" I turned to Aunt Shell and Uncle Mark.

"He knew you were in trouble, and he knew he had to talk if you were going to make it," Uncle Mark explained.

"You can thank this young lady right here for telling us to come down to the hollow in the first place," Aunt Shell said, pulling someone from behind her. And there, standing before me, was my very best friend for life, Angel Always Swope!

"I called over to your house," Angel explained, "so we could talk about the ghost some more. When your aunt told me how first Nelson was missin' and then you and Zack, I put two and two together and figured out what happened."

"So you told Aunt Shell where we were?" I asked.

Angel frowned. "Well, not at first. I was worried about gettin' into trouble, but then I got to worryin' about you even more, so I called the firehouse."

"The firehouse?" I croaked. "But how did you know there was a fire?"

"I didn't," Angel admitted. "I jes' figured that the police force bein' so busy huntin' and all, they might not get here very quick. I knew the firemen would, 'cause my uncle Brad is a volunteer and he's the best fireman around."

"How did you know to come?" I asked, turning to Uncle Mark.

"Angel reconsidered and decided to give us a call back. She said she would only tell us what she knew, if we promised to take her with us."

"I would've gone crazy for sure, jes' sittin'

and waitin' and not knowin' what was goin' on," Angel exclaimed.

She winked at me through those big blue glasses of hers, and I finally understood what Angel had been trying to tell me about the "wonderful power of love." I could see now how it had given Nelson the power to talk and Angel the power to risk her daddy's temper to save our lives.

As we watched Zack being carried into the ambulance on a stretcher, he nodded in our direction. He had an oxygen mask on his face, so it was hard to see his expression, but I could tell he was smiling. Angel blushed and waved. Mr. Brisson came over to tell us that they thought Zack would be all right, but he would need to go to the hospital.

Miss Loop had her arms around her brother, who seemed to be dazed. After the ambulance sped away to the hospital, we sat down in the weeds and watched the firemen trying to bring the fire under control.

I sat beside Nelson, feeling happy and sad at the same time. I was sad about the Loops having to see their father's factory burn down, but I couldn't help smiling at my brother. He didn't say anything, but smiled back at me.

"The window, Jenna's at the window." I kept whispering the words over and over, unable to believe that I had really heard them. I was so busy staring at Nelson's face, I didn't pay much attention to the walking stick in his hands. He must have been playing with the marble in the snake's mouth, sticking his finger in and trying to push the marble out between the carved wooden fangs, because suddenly it fell out onto the grass.

With all that the Loops had lost, I was horrified to see that the only treasure they had left, their father's walking stick, had been broken. Before I could take the stick away from Nelson, he pulled on the snake's head, causing it to flip back. Then he tilted the cane over and began to shake it. We were speechless as a stream of sparkling jewels poured out onto the grass.

"Land's alive, it's Daddy's treasure!" Miss Loop cried. "His rainy-day treasure! He always told us he had a treasure hidden away for a rainy day, but we never did find it, till now!"

It was a real treasure, with rubies, and diamonds, just like you see on TV. Speaking of

TV, a truck from the local TV station pulled up. The evening news team had come to cover the fire. And that's how Angel and I got ourselves on the six o'clock news.

Angel said she wished she had known they were coming, because she would have "put some mousse stuff" on her hair. I thought she looked fine. I was the one who was a mess. My face was smudgy and my hair was sticking up and I was grinning like a fool.

We were all smiling as we looked down at the Loops's "rainy-day treasure." Miss Loop was saying how Irwin wouldn't need to go into the county hospital now, and that she could buy back her "holler, " where she intended to put up a new house.

Angel not only looked good, but she sounded good, too. She looked straight into the camera, and in her best TV voice, she explained what brought us to the hollow in the first place—our wish to shock Nelson into talking. (Of course she was saying this for her father's benefit, but he still took away her TV watching for two weeks.) The cameras panned back to the burning building and then to the Loops and their newfound treasure.

The last shot was of Nelson sitting beside me, laughing. It was a wonderful laugh, not loud or screechy, but soft and gentle and full of distinction. Just the kind of laugh that my best friend for life and I knew it would be, the kind of laugh that gave us both goose bumps, lots and lots of wonderful goose bumps.